Lilac Skully and the Carriage of Lost Souls

BOOK #2
IN THE SUPERNATURAL ADVENTURES
OF LILAC SKULLY

Lilac Skully and the Carriage of Lost Souls

AMY CESARI

1.

The State of Skully Manor

When Lilac awoke, her bed felt like it was turned around the wrong way. She sat up and braced her arms on the mattress. She was upstairs in her own room, where she hadn't slept in years. Her hand reached back and felt a throbbing lump on her head.

"Lilac Skully, beaned with a candlestick in the foyer," she mumbled as she began to recall bits of what had happened last night.

The manor was still and silent. Something in the atmosphere felt different, and not just because Lilac was on the second floor instead of hiding in the maid's quarters on the first floor. Three of the ghosts of Skully Manor were gone, and Lilac could feel their absence in the air. She inhaled slowly and deeply, her eyes nearly closed as she tried to sense a rooty, darker note from the usual pale, sweet, haunted scent of her home. But it wasn't there.

She lay back down and stared at the cracks in the plaster ceiling. Funny, she thought, how things change so quickly once you see them in a new way.

It had only been a few days since she tried to get rid of the ghosts by performing a séance. And now, she didn't want the ghosts to leave. In fact, she would do anything to protect them.

She sat up and rubbed the bulbous aching knot on the back of her head. She grumbled.

"Well," she said to her cat, Casper, who was curled up at the foot of the bed. "I guess I'll go make some tea." She stroked his sandy, striped fur a few times. He stretched to wake up and then followed.

The manor had been robbed two nights in a row, and the aftermath was everywhere. Lilac and Casper stepped carefully over the trip wire that she'd set up to stop the burglars. A pet cemetery grave marker attached to a rope that Lilac had flung through the foyer lay tipped on its side, its left wing broken in half, the marble floor cracked beneath. A string of spent firecrackers sat atop a black burn mark in the carpet. The door that led down to the cellar was smashed through the middle, the wood splintered out dramatically.

Lilac tiptoed past the damage and went into the kitchen. She put the teakettle on the stove and set out some fish for Casper. She took out a box of crackers and a gigantic jar of generic peanut butter and grape jam. The teakettle whistled, and she poured her tea. She sat quietly for a few moments and crunched her peanut butter, jam, and crackers.

She wasn't sure what to do next. But she knew the danger had not passed, and now, most unsettling, she knew it had been looming over her and the ghosts of the manor for quite some time.

She went to the shelf in the pantry where she kept her books, and pulled out a spiral-bound notebook, *The Diary of Lilac Skully,* and a pen from the kitchen drawer. Lilac glanced over what she'd already written, then tore out all of the pages, ripped them in half, and threw them in the trash. So much had changed. After tapping the pen against her bottom lip a couple of times, Lilac began to write.

Well, it's been an interesting couple of days. I found out that ghost hunters have been trying to capture the ghosts here at Skully Manor for a long time. They're from a place called Black, Black, and Gremory, and I think they might have something to do with my father's disappearance!

And now they've broken into the house two nights in a row. It's been horrible. The first night, they kidnapped Archie, Milly's brother, the little boy ghost that haunted the halls upstairs...

Archie. A wave of guilt washed over her. It still felt like her fault, like she hadn't taken action quickly enough to help him. She looked at the clock. Nearly ten in the morning. Archie would've never let her sleep till ten upstairs. He would've come to haunt the doorway with a game of jacks or cards or one of his other spooky tricks. But he wasn't there this morning. And she missed him.

It was true that Lilac had been terrified of the ghosts of Skully Manor for most of her childhood. But now, things were different. Lilac and the ghosts were friends. And they were all in danger.

Lilac continued writing.

It turns out Archie isn't the first ghost they've kidnapped here. Milly says they captured a spirit called the Blue Lady from the garden. It was a couple of years ago.

Then they broke in AGAIN last night and tried to capture the rest of the ghosts! We thought we were ready for them, but we barely held them off. And they almost got away with everyone—Bram and Milly and Mr. Fright were all trapped in those orbs until...

Lilac stopped again and sipped her tea. Mr. Fright. For her entire life and until just that past day or two—Mr. Fright had been the ghost that scared Lilac the most. He was notorious for his dislike of little girls, and because Lilac was a little girl, Mr. Fright took extra delight in scaring her. But last night, Mr. Fright and Lilac had worked together to defend Skully Manor. Soon after, his spirit passed into the light. And thinking about it now, Lilac felt an unsettling sense of loss.

She wasn't quite sure what to call it, because Mr. Fright had already been a ghost. He didn't die. He was already dead. But his spirit had moved on. The other ghosts said he'd resolved what had kept him haunting, and although it was bittersweet, she shouldn't feel too sad. But she did.

Lilac continued writing on a new line, not finishing the previous sentence.

I don't really know how to explain it. But Mr. Fright's spirit disappeared last night, right in the entrance of the foyer. Milly said he's in another realm beyond, and that he's not coming back, at least not here. He's gone. And I never thought I'd say this, but I think I'm going to miss him.

She closed the notebook and fought back tears by

scrunching up her nose and eyes and throat as much as she could. But it didn't work.

The entire house sat in a heavy fog of mourning. Everything felt different. Skully Manor was that much more empty, that much more alone. The walls creaked with less enthusiasm. The warped wooden frame sunk down further, more sullen. There hadn't been any rattling doors, disembodied voices, or grim cackles in the night. How peculiar it was without Mr. Fright. Lilac had slept so well.

Lilac counted on her fingers, slowly as she went back and forth between her two hands, twice. Her father had been gone now for sixteen days. Half a month. The pale complexion of her face grew more ashen, and the dark, heavy feeling in her stomach began to churn. Lilac knew her father was in trouble. And she missed him. Terribly. She wondered how much longer she could make it on her own.

The break-ins, the captured ghosts, and the disappearance of her father were linked to something larger and more sinister than she'd allowed herself to admit. She was in danger. They all were. And Lilac, only nine-and-three-quarters, knew it was up to her to figure it out.

Lilac drank her tea slowly, till the last bit in the cup

was cold.

"I haven't seen Milly yet this morning. I wonder where she is?" Lilac said to herself. She hopped off the stool. She poured some more hot water and carried her teacup and saucer back into the foyer.

"Milly?" she called out, but Milly didn't respond. Lilac went back upstairs to the hall on the second floor, where Milly, the Little Girl Ghost, was known to haunt. But Milly wasn't there.

"Milly?" Lilac shouted up the stairs to the third floor, then took one step up at a time, making sure not to spill her tea. "Milly?" Lilac said at the top of the stairs. She flicked the switch at the end of the hall, and the lights blinked on.

She tried to remember the last time she'd been up there. Possibly never, as she'd avoided the haunted third floor of the house for her entire life, and she didn't have any idea what was behind the closed doors.

At the end of the hall, Lilac set down her tea and pulled back a damask curtain with a cloud of dust. She gasped. Through a distorted pane of glass, she saw the ocean. Silvery glints of light accented the waves in the distance. From her vantage point, she could see over the entire town that sat between Skully Manor and the sea. She spotted the downtown clock tower and the steeple of the white church up the hill. She could even look into the yards of her neighbors. She never knew she could see these things before, right here, from the third floor of her own home. She had missed so much by hiding away downstairs. Afraid of the ghosts. Afraid of everything. She wondered what other magnificent things were out there.

"It's beautiful, isn't it?" a quiet voice said.

"Milly!" Lilac replied, "I was hoping I'd find you up here."

Milly wore a fancy pale blue party outfit, complete with ruffly socks, patent leather shoes, and a large droopy bow on her sandy blonde hair.

"Good morning, Lilac," Milly said.

"Good morning Milly, um, yeah..." Lilac looked out of the window again and motioned to the ocean view. "It's amazing."

"Archie and I used to play here a lot." Milly sighed. "It's just not the same without him."

Lilac looked out of the window again. She didn't know what to say. She wanted to tell Milly she'd find a way to get Archie and her father back. But it felt like a lie. She didn't know how. Or where to start. Or if it was even possible.

Lilac looked back down the hall at the row of closed doors. She was curious to see what was inside them, but she hesitated. It felt more like Milly's house than hers since Milly had haunted there for more than a hundred years.

"What's in these rooms?" Lilac finally asked.

"Bedrooms," Milly shrugged. "And a washroom there," she said. "It's blue," she added, as her gaze dropped to the floor.

"Blue?" Lilac asked, and Milly nodded.

Lilac went to look. She twisted the rusty handle on the washroom door.

She gasped. "All turquoise?" Lilac said in disbelief. Everything in the third-floor bathroom including the walls, the tile, the porcelain toilet, the sink, the claw-footed tub, the leaded glass light fixture, the curtains, and the translucent, shriveled bar of soap—was a pale, ethereal turquoise blue. Lilac had never seen anything like it. Delighted, she went to the next door in the hall and opened it.

It was dusty and musty and covered with cobwebs, and a faint smell of flowery perfume hung in the air.

"Oh. Milly!" Lilac gasped. "Look at this beautiful room! It's got butterflies!"

Lilac opened the curtains to let in more light. There was blue and green butterfly wallpaper on the walls. Tiny flecks of silver dotted their wings. Some of the paper was ripped, falling, or stained yellow, but it was beautiful to Lilac. The room had sat in darkness for nearly a decade, yet the butterflies looked like they had been flittering joyously on the walls the entire time.

Lilac grew more excited as she opened doors and cupboards and closets. It was overwhelming for her to see it all at once, even as she took her time. There were clocks and books and clothes and lamps and cross-stitched things on the walls. Surprises popped up wherever she laid her eyes.

Another bedroom on the third floor had stately green striped wallpaper. There was a stone fireplace, some moldy old leather furniture, and the ancient scent of tobacco. A floor-to-ceiling shelf was filled with books about war that looked boring, and a taxidermy buck with massive antlers hung on the wall.

"He really was a fascinating creature," Milly said as she saw Lilac staring at the mounted deer's head. "He haunted here for a short while anyway, before he moved on," she added.

Lilac smiled.

"Listen to this!" Milly said as she floated towards a wooden cabinet radio.

There was a whir and a crackle, and the radio started to play. Milly had a knack for radios—and a history of it, too. She could do typical ghostly things, like speak through them and disrupt the frequencies. But she also loved to play music, mixing up different stations to create strange new melodies.

Two songs interchanged through an old, tinny-sounding speaker, switching from station to station to the beat. It was part ragtime, part wheedly-deedly clarinet jazz, and Lilac Skully burst out laughing at the sound of the playful, silly horn.

Milly began to dance, and Lilac did, too. The girls both pretended to play the piano during the ragtime part. Then, they played the horns and bloopy stand-up bass in the jazz. Lilac danced and twirled and laughed till her ribs hurt.

One of the songs came to an end and went to a commercial. Lilac giggled and sat on the floor to catch her breath. Milly began to flicker in and out of view, running low on energy from operating the radio.

"I'm going to fade out for a bit." Milly said to Lilac.

"See you soon." Lilac said, and Milly disappeared into the hall.

Casper walked in to see what was going on. "Mrow?" he asked, as he thought it was unusual to find Lilac on the third floor.

Lilac pet her cat's head and sat with him for a moment. Then she got up and went back downstairs to the second floor, making sure to turn off the lights and close the doors behind her. Casper followed.

She went down the hall to her father's room. She

could only remember one other time—just a few hours ago—when she'd been in there before. She had seen her mother's photograph. And she wanted to see it again.

Lilac crept in quietly and sat on the edge of the bed. She stared into her mother's eyes in the photograph on the bedside table. She wondered if her mother had sat right there. And was that her mother's mirrored vanity, too? It must have been. Most of the furniture was in the house when the Skully family bought it four generations ago.

Lilac went to the vanity and sat down on the tufted stool. She stared at her reflection in the mirror. She tried to see a resemblance to her mother's photograph. And although she looked almost exactly like her mother, with shockingly light blonde hair and round gray eyes, Lilac didn't see the similarity. She saw an odd little girl with a wild, untamed, lonely look on her face. She turned away.

She opened one of the drawers on the vanity with an instinctive fidget. She froze. A brush, a comb, a tube of lipstick, and a few other boxes of makeup sat in an enameled tray. The brush had strands of coarse white-blonde hair wrapped around it. Her mother's hair.

She went cold. It had to be her mother's. Who else's? Lilac's hand did not move from the knob of the drawer. Her eyes locked on the strands of hair.

Every cupboard and corner of the house she'd explored that day unveiled curiosities, antiquities, and heirlooms, things that belonged to her mother, her grandmother, and her great-grandmother. But she had not expected to find this, her mother's hair, still wrapped in the brush. It seemed as shocking to Lilac as if she had come across her mother's hand or her skeleton or her skull for that matter, like Lilac had opened a mummy's tomb in a far corner of the world.

Lilac shut the drawer and stood up from the vanity. She left her father's room and closed the door behind her. She walked as calmly as she could through the halls and back into her room. She wanted to cry, but the dull ache of loneliness made crying impossible. She lay face down on her bed in silence. There was no use in feeling sad. She had been so young when her mother died, that she couldn't remember anything about her at all, even when she used her imagination. Her mother was gone.

And she knew her father wasn't going to return "quickly," as he said when speaking through the ghost communication equipment not more than two days ago. There was something very wrong. She knew it. He was in trouble.

Lilac suddenly sat straight up.

"The equipment!" she shrieked. She'd hidden it after her father spoke through it and warned her about the intruders. And maybe she could use it to reach him again, to find out what was going on, and to get him back.

Lilac scurried downstairs. Once in the kitchen, she pulled up the loose floorboard in the pantry and laid on her stomach. With a lot of huffing and puffing, she got the pieces of the communication device back up into the kitchen and down into her father's lab.

She plugged in the machines and connected the wires between the various antennas and sockets, just as she thought they were before.

"Well," she said out loud, "here goes."

Lilac pushed the power button and flicked the "on" switch.

Glunk.

The monitor blinked a few times to static. The machine whirred.

"Hello?" Lilac said into the small microphone. She turned a few of the knobs on the control panel. One of them adjusted the static into big green stripes, moving across the screen hypnotically. "Hello?" Lilac repeated. "Is there anybody in there? Father? Can you hear me?" Lilac said again into the machine. She tried different combinations of knobs and wires and controls, then found a loose wire and plugged it into a socket where it seemed to fit.

A deafening screech came out of a speaker. She covered her ears with both hands, then removed one of them to turn the volume down.

Then, she heard the deep voice of a man. For a split second, Lilac felt a surge of excitement. But it was not her father's voice.

"What are you gonna do with her boss?" the man's voice said. "Then what?"

Lilac sat perfectly still and did not make a sound.

A different voice spoke. It mumbled. It had a lower tone, much darker sounding than the first. Lilac could not distinguish the words.

"You're going to bring her down there?" the first man said in disbelief. "You're kidding! I won't even go down there! Boss, with all due respect, I mean... that's... that's crazy, she's... she's alive..." he said emphasizing the last two words.

The unintelligible man laughed in a way that made Lilac shiver, then spoke again. She still couldn't understand the words he said, but his sinister voice chilled her to the bone.

"I dunno about this, boss, I just don't know," the first man said.

"Lilac?" Lilac heard behind her. It was Milly.

"Uh... yeah?" Lilac said back.

Before Milly could speak again, the voice on the

speaker came back.

"Did you hear that?" the man's voice said. The blank monitor screen flashed to green stripes, then to static.

Then the faces of two men blinked into fuzzy view. Lilac looked at the monitor and gasped as she covered her mouth.

"Well!" said the dark, nasty voice of the man Lilac had not been able to understand. "Speak of the devil!" he laughed.

Lilac gasped, and in a flurry, turned off the equipment and unplugged the wires, her hands and arms shaking as she yanked out the cords.

"Oh my god!" Lilac said frantically. "They saw me!"

2.

HUNGER SETS IN

L ilac ran back upstairs to her room. She threw a pillow over her head and screamed into the mattress.

"That was so stupid!" she yelled. They had seen her. They were coming for her. She was doomed.

"Miss Skully?"

She heard a quiet, familiar voice at the door. She peeked out from beneath the pillow. It was Bram, the butler, one of the two ghosts that still haunted the manor. He was dressed in a neatly tailored suit with vest and tails, just as you would expect the ghost of a Victorian butler to wear.

Lilac didn't sit up, and held the pillow back tightly over her head.

Bram hesitated in the doorway. "Miss Skully," he said again as he floated into her room. "I, err. Um..." he stuttered. He coughed slightly, took the white gloves out of his front pocket, fanned himself, and spoke again. "I believe, um... " he shook his head and sighed. "It's going to be... well, alright." he finally said, and then stopped talking.

"I can't believe I did something so stupid." Lilac choked out the words. "They're gonna come back now for you and Milly, and it's my fault," she said with a wail.

"We were already in danger, Miss Skully, and I'm afraid it's only a matter of time before they return either way," Bram said to her. "And you were quite clever last night, I wanted to mention that to you. And thank you."

Lilac didn't reply. Bram continued when he came up with something more to say.

"And I dare say, Miss Skully, if they come back, I know I can speak for Milly and myself that we'd need you on our side again."

"WHEN they come back!" she cried, her voice muffled underneath the pillow.

Bram shook his head. "Lilac, dear," he said.

She listened but did not remove the pillow from over her head.

"We're in this together, as residents of Skully Manor." Bram said. "Dead or alive, we can't give up, not yet, not now, not ever." He gave a short nod, as if it were final.

Lilac wiped her eyes. She sat up on the bed.

"So what do I do now?" she asked him. "How can I get my father back? And Archie? And how can I make sure they don't get you and Milly too?"

"I wish I knew, Miss Skully," he said. "But it may be time to take some action," he paused, "or get some help," He cleared his throat. "There's someone I can contact on the spirit side, someone who may be of assistance." He sighed. "I don't think you're safe here, anymore, Miss Skully."

"I haven't been safe here for a long time," she said back. Bram looked as if he was going to interject, but Lilac added, "And I don't have anywhere else to go."

Bram stopped. It was true.

Lilac sat on the edge of the bed for a few moments. Then she quietly made her way down into the cellar once more.

She went into her father's lab. A sinking feeling came over her as she recalled how foolish she had been. It was hot like the searing melt of embarrassment where you want to disappear forever or erase the memory from your mind. What had she been thinking, setting up the equipment and trying to contact her father?

A sad, soft voice called from behind her.

"Hi Lilac," the voice said. It was Milly.

"Hi Milly," Lilac returned.

"I'm sorry?" Milly said hesitantly, like she was asking a question.

"Why?" Lilac asked.

"They   heard   me   come   through   the   ghost

communicator," Milly said. "It was my fault."

"It's okay," Lilac shrugged and squatted down, hugging her knees. "It was my fault, too, and it sounds like they're planning to come back, anyway."

"I miss Archie," Milly continued, her face scrunched up as she tried to stifle her tears.

"I know," Lilac said. "I do, too. And..." She felt a lump in her throat. "I'm not going to give up," she said, even though Lilac had no idea what to do. "I'll get Archie back, and my father." She nodded. "Somehow."

Milly tried to calm herself again and sat down, sniffling on the floor in her pale blue party dress.

"Well," Lilac looked around her father's lab. "The first time they came in here, they were looking for papers and equipment."

"And ghosts!" Milly said.

"And, ghosts," Lilac agreed. "And we know they're from a place called Black, Black, and Gremory." Milly nodded once in response, her big swirling eyes looked up at Lilac.

"I bet there are more clues in here somewhere," Lilac said, "I think I even saw an address on a letter, in that file of papers that seemed important." Lilac tried to recall where she had put that file. "If I can find out where Black Black, and Gremory is, maybe I can find my father."

"And Archie?" Milly asked with a twinge of teary hope.

"And Archie." Lilac said with confidence. "I think they were kidnapped by the same people... I'm pretty sure," she added with less certainty.

Lilac turned to the file cabinets. She began to search methodically, starting in one cabinet and looking at each piece of paper. Just as she thought, there was a letter from Forsyth Gremory with an address at the bottom. She set it aside with anything else that caught her eye, but there wasn't much.

She was about to shut the drawer when she saw a file folder that had fallen off the rails in the back. It looked older than the other files. Something was written on the label in pale blue ink. Lilac didn't recognize the bubbly, soft handwriting. She picked it up and paused.

"Lenore Skully," she read off the folder, ever so quietly. Her lip began to tremble, and her voice was cracking and squeaking out the words as she read the rest of the writing. "Notes and Musings."

She felt tears well up in her eyes.

"Who's Lenore?" Milly asked.

"My mother." Lilac responded, her voice gurgling and choking out over a block of emotion.

"Oh!" Milly said almost cheerfully. "Lenore. Lenore. Lenore..." Milly repeated the name a few times, thinking to herself. "Sounds familiar. I think I remember her," she said, looking over to the side a bit and down. "But maybe it was something from a poem? I'm... I'm not quite sure. My memories can be a bit fuzzy. But I do think she was a very kind lady, Lilac. And I do think I remember her." Milly explained.

"What happened to her after she..." Lilac stopped.

Milly shook her head. She didn't know.

"Why are you..." Lilac stopped again. She wanted to ask why Milly was a ghost that still haunted the house, and why her mom wasn't. But she didn't ask. Milly seemed to know what she meant, anyway.

"It's complicated," Milly answered vaguely, "and I'm not entirely sure myself." Milly looked thoughtful and added, "If I knew, maybe I wouldn't..." she trailed off and stopped.

Lilac knew what Milly meant. Maybe she wouldn't still be there, haunting the same home for a century. Lilac liked having Milly in the house, and it made her sad to think that someday she might not be around.

Lilac opened the folder with her mother's name and saw a slim notebook inside. There were quite a few pages written in the same handwriting. She'd never read anything written by her mother, but she hoped it would be wonderful.

She collected the other papers that seemed relevant

to her father's whereabouts. Not much, other than the letters between Black, Black, and Gremory, her father, and various law firms that she didn't understand. But she'd found the address, and though it didn't feel like much at all, it was the only clue she had.

Lilac brought the paperwork upstairs to her room and set it aside. She wanted to read what her mother wrote, but it still felt too strange.

Instead, she spent the afternoon filling out her overdue correspondence schoolwork as quickly as she could, and then lost herself in reading *Charlotte's Web.*

In the early evening, she made herself a cup of tea and some crackers with peanut butter and jam. Casper joined her, and she went to the nearly-empty fridge for the open can of fish. There was only a small bite left. She went to the pantry for another can.

She opened the can, but there wasn't fish inside.

"Dolmas!" she said to herself and shook her head. There had been a few dusty unlabeled cans on the back shelf that she thought were mackerel. But it turns out they were dolmas, a Greek delicacy made with seasoned rice wrapped in grape leaves.

"Shoot," she muttered.

"I'll have to bring up some more cat food from the basement," she explained to him as he licked his plate clean.

Just two days ago, she wouldn't have gone down into the cellar if she could help it, and certainly not alone. But now, things were different. Not just because she was friends with the ghosts, but because Mr. Fright had passed on, and the basement wasn't so scary anymore.

Lilac flipped the switches and pulled strings on each of the flickering, dim bulbs that lit different sections of the cellar, but there were no cans of cat food there, either.

"Uh oh," she muttered as she went back upstairs. "Bram?" She called out.

"Miss Skully?" Bram appeared at the upstairs landing.

"Have you seen any cat food? Any fish or meat that I can feed Casper?" Since Bram had been the butler of Skully Manor for over one hundred years, he had a knack for knowing where things were.

Bram paused and looked up for a moment, his hands clasped behind his back.

"I'm afraid not, Miss Skully," he shook his head, and Lilac could see bits of ghostly dust fall around his translucent, glowing apparition.

Bram cleared his throat, "I'm concerned that your supplies are running low," he said.

Lilac did not respond.

"At some point, Miss Skully, you're going to have to leave..."

Lilac cut him off, not wanting to make a big deal about it, although it had been months, if not a year or more, since Lilac had left the manor.

"Well, do you know where there's any money, then?" She asked him. "If I have to go to the store, fine. But I can't do that without money."

Bram thought. "There's a safe in your father's closet with quite a bit of cash. However, I don't know the combination."

Lilac's mouth twisted up and she squinted one eye. Bram pondered a bit more, and then spoke again.

"There are some long-forgotten bills folded in one of your father's coat pockets," he said to Lilac. "Hanging in his closet," he added. "The brown tweed one with the mismatched elbow patches..." he said more specifically.

Lilac's eyes lit up. That sounded like a much easier place to start than breaking into her father's safe.

"And," Bram added as Lilac passed by on the upstairs landing, "there's an old brass piggy bank on the library shelf with a bit of spare change."

"Thanks a lot!" Lilac said as she went back into her father's room.

She opened his closet, and a wave of his aura wafted out. She stopped with her hand on the doorknob. She had never been in her father's closet. The scent and the personal nature of his empty clothes, old shoes, hats, and belongings overwhelmed her. She had been angry at him for leaving her alone so long. Not just for the past few weeks—but for her entire lifetime. But now, being amongst his things, she suddenly felt awful that she had been so upset. So selfish. He'd been in deep trouble and likely quite lonely. For how long? She knew the answer. Since her mother's death.

She broke herself from a trance of swirling memories and rummaged for the coat Bram had mentioned. She found it, and exactly as he had told her, there were a few folded bills and coins tucked in the pocket.

"Twenty-seven dollars," she counted, "and seventeen cents," She nodded her head, closed the closet, and hurried out of the room.

"Thanks! It's enough for now," she said to Bram on the landing and went back down to the kitchen.

Casper was waiting as patiently as he could, next to his empty plate, sitting upright with his paws poised politely.

"I'm sorry, Casper," she told him, "I messed up." She shook her head. "There's no more cat food down there."

He meowed and asked again.

"I'm so sorry," Lilac said. "The sun's already going down, and..." Lilac gulped, "I don't want to be out at night," she told him. She didn't. She knew that leaving the house in the daytime was going to be scary enough. She didn't want to make it any worse by adding the darkness and all of the creatures like bears and cougars and kidnappers and vampire bats and other things that come out at night.

"I'll go out first thing in the morning." She gave her cat some extra pets and rubbed his belly, hoping it would help him forget about food for the night. She gave him an extra-large bowl of water.

"As soon as it's daylight," she nodded. "I think it'll be safer that way," she reasoned to her cat.

Lilac finished her crackers and ate the opened can of dolmas. She put on a kettle and sat at the counter, staring blankly, worrying about what might happen when she left the house. She went to the pantry to take stock of her food supply.

She had seen three economy-sized boxes of crackers and a three-gallon bucket of generic peanut butter in the basement. That alone could last for months. There were eight orange sodas in the fridge. The pantry held even more food, the five cans of dolmas, twelve different tins of tea, two cans of string beans, one of chili, and an ancient spice rack with various spices. Sufficient, she thought.

The whistle blew on the kettle. Lilac poured her tea.

Slowly and without spilling, she carried the cup and saucer back up to her room.

Once in her room, she continued to read *Charlotte's Web*.

"Miss Skully?" Bram called from the hallway a few minutes later.

"Come in, Bram," Lilac responded.

"I'm sorry to disturb you, but I've got bad news."

Lilac's stomach sank like she had swallowed a rock. She tried to guess what that might be but just drew a cold, dull, blank because there were too many terrible options to choose from. She looked at him to go on and tell her.

Bram continued. "A white van has just pulled up again outside. Cleverly hidden and almost out of sight in the shrubbery, but thankfully, Milly was gazing out of the window and saw it arrive."

Lilac gulped and fought off a feeling of impending doom. They were back. It was Black, Black, and Gremory.

3.

Just a Short Walk

Lilac was unable to sleep that night. She'd done her best to barricade the basement door that had been torn off its hinges a few nights ago, and her family sword was tucked right there under the bed. Bram and Milly even agreed to keep watch overnight. But she didn't feel safe. Restless, she tossed and turned.

Eventually, she must've fallen asleep, because Casper woke her at the first rays of dawn.

"Mrow?" he scratched politely and hungrily on her bedroom door.

"Cat food," she said as she sat straight up and got out of bed without hesitation. She looked out the window and peered down the street. The white van was still there. There was a foggy, misty morning dew on it. She was certain it had been parked there all night.

"Mrow?" Casper said again as she unlocked her bedroom door.

"I'm going to go to the store right now," she told him calmly. "It's just a short walk," she reassured him.

But it wasn't. Skully Manor was on the outskirts

of town, on the edge of a thick, dark forest at the foot of the coastal mountains. It was over a mile and a half to the nearest store, which might even take thirty or forty minutes to walk each way. She put on her sneakers over woolen tights, corduroy pants, and her thickest sweater. She put the money she'd found safely inside her backpack.

"Bram?" she called out in the foyer.

"Good morning, Miss Skully," he said as he appeared from the bedroom suite on the other side of the landing, which he was fond of haunting.

"There was no activity last night. I hope you slept well," he added.

"Thanks," she replied, and left out the part about being too worried to sleep. "I'm walking to the store," she said confidently, then swallowed a pang of panic and fear that made her feel like she was going to turn inside out.

"You'll be alright, Miss Skully," Bram said calmly, sensing her nervousness.

"Mrow?" Casper asked again.

"It's just a short walk," she said back to Casper, talking herself into it and mustering her courage together. "I'll be back soon."

She went to the kitchen and got the key to Skully Manor out of the drawer. She took a gulp of water from the tap and promised herself a hot cup of tea as soon as she got back.

She walked confidently to the kitchen door and undid the various locks. She pulled it open a crack and paused. Then she slipped out into the cold, damp autumn air. With her manor skeleton key, she locked the door shut from the outside, and then trotted silently through the shadows.

The backyard of Skully Manor had been beautifully landscaped a hundred years ago. It had raised beds, ornate concrete statuary, and plots overflowing with flowers, berries, and herbs. But now, the yard of Skully Manor was an overgrown monstrosity, the kind of garden that left you in awe of Mother Nature's wild desire to overcome and take root. There were towering green and purple thistles with needle-sharp spikes a good three inches long. Vines twisted and squeezed concrete pillars, their persistence paying off as the stones eventually began to crack, and the roots took hold in the rock. The branches of the old oak tree jutted out at dangerous angles and looked as if they might snap under their own weight. An angel statue sat headless, its head rolled off to the side on the ground, looking up quizzically as Lilac ran past.

Lilac unlatched the garden gate and opened it a

crack.

Creeeeak, it went, then *cling!* it chimed as she tried to close it softly. She stepped through and peered cautiously this way and that, in both directions down the dirt road on the side of Skully Manor.

Lilac darted across the street and into a vacant lot. She ducked between two massive clumps of weeds and stopped to look back at her home. It wasn't often that she saw Skully Manor from the outside. She tilted her head. It had been months since she'd been outside at all, maybe even longer, other than to bring the trash to the curb or pick some catnip from the old herb garden, or take her correspondence coursework to and from the post box.

Skully Manor was a strange looking house. Dark, she thought, and empty. Without a glint of color other than the pale grayish green weeds in the yard. It was three stories tall, with an even taller tower rising up from the middle. The tower was narrow, and its roof loomed high and skinny above everything else in the neighborhood. Enormous amounts of ornate trim—wood, cast iron, brick, stone, cement—decorated every nook, cranny, and corner in a dilapidated, dull manner, tilting slightly in different directions. The steep, concave mansard roof shot downwards and out at a droopy, sad looking angle, like tears rolling off of cheeks. And the front dormer windows of the house looked like eyes to Lilac, the way they stuck out and were rounded at the top. Frightened eyes, she thought, surprised eyes that could not move or run, but just stared blankly out at the world, waiting helplessly for whatever might come next.

Lilac turned away from her house and darted into the vacant lot. She cut through the back, hiding amongst the neglected weeds and thistles. Once she was sure she was out of sight of the white van, she hopped onto the sidewalk.

She was nervous. Every sound, twig, or tweet of the birds startled her and set her heart racing faster as her footsteps quickened. But once the initial shock wore off and she was well on her way, she realized how good it felt to be out in the fresh morning air. It felt cold and crisp in her lungs, like a burst of energy. It felt good. She hadn't seen anyone yet at all. No one was chasing her.

It smelled so much different than the stagnant, dusty, ghostly, moldy air in Skully Manor. The sun was up, but it was early enough that most people were still in bed. Lilac had the neighborhood to herself. She listened to the sound and the rhythm of her footsteps. She watched the slight mist of her breath go in and out in front of her.

She put a bit of a skip in her step and began to feel the freedom of being out on her own. She liked the different personalities of people's houses, how some of them were so bright and cheery, with things that regular houses and ordinary families had, kids' toys and colorful rain boots on the porch. It was a typical neighborhood, she thought, that wasn't haunted. She sighed. These houses were not like Skully Manor. Her house was ancient, and almost all of these houses looked much newer and more simply built. Skully Manor was brown and gray and the color of dust and ghosts, with spiked, fierce-looking wrought iron garnishes on the top of the roof and front wall. These homes were white, yellow, beige, and bright blue. They had colorful flowers, she noted, not thistles, and the plants were green. Where Skully Manor had weeds, other houses had neatly mowed lawns.

By the time Lilac could see the bright lights of the 24-hour convenience market up ahead, she was smiling and enjoying her walk, breaking into a light sweat, and breathing in lungfuls of sweet, clean air, stretching her legs and imagination. Her smile turned solemn and purposeful as she went through the electric sliding door of the shop.

"*Bing Bong!*" said the door as Lilac stepped through.

Lilac rehearsed her story in her head. Just in case anyone asked, her father had influenza. Terrible influenza. That's why she had to go to the store all alone.

She grabbed two shopping baskets and found the

cat food section quickly enough. She loaded one basket with two bags of kibble and the other with as many cans of fish as she could carry. She wandered to the packaged people-food. Her pantry had enough to last her a while, it was true. But she was getting sick of crackers and peanut butter, and as the weather grew colder and more wintery, she wished she had something hot to eat. She filled up the two baskets to capacity with twenty-two packets of single-serve dehydrated noodles. Chicken flavor. At an excellent price, she noted.

She pretended to look at the shampoo for a while and rehearsed the story in her head. If she had to, she'd say she was contagious with the flu, and that everyone needed to stay far away from her. She began to feel her nerves jangle, and she swallowed hard. Her heart began to pound.

As purposefully as she could, she took her items to the counter, and tried not to shake as she unloaded the twenty-two crinkly packets of noodles, two by two. The checker was a young woman who, to Lilac's relief, could not care less why a child of nine-and-three-quarters was out by herself at dawn buying cat food and twenty-two packets of dehydrated noodles.

"Seventeen dollars and forty-two cents," the lady said. Lilac handed the woman the twenty dollar bill and took back her change. The woman helped her put the noodles and most of the canned fish into a plastic shopping bag. Lilac loaded one of the large kibble bags and the rest of the fish into her backpack. She held the other bag of kibble under her arm.

She politely thanked the woman, who gave her a nonchalant and disinterested, "You're welcome," and Lilac hurried out of the store.

"*Bing Bong!*" said the door as Lilac stepped out.

Her feet felt light as she trotted home. That hadn't been as bad as she'd thought! Even fun... maybe... to go out to the store. She smiled. No one had noticed or cared or pointed out anything strange about her. Dare she say—she'd even fit in? Just like anyone else who pops into the store to get a few things. She skipped back to the other side to see which side of the sidewalk she preferred.

She had only gone a few blocks, but the weight of the bags of kibble and the canned food and noodles was already feeling heavier. She shifted her load a bit and continued, looking up at the sycamore trees and noticing that it was that point of the morning where the bird songs reached a crescendo. They had been tweeting a bit on her way to the store, but now, the birds were singing in full force, rejoicing in the freedom and freshness of the new day. She picked up her pace again out of excitement.

After a few minutes more, she noticed that the birds had stopped tweeting. She gave a quick glance behind her and felt a twinge of paranoia, like someone was following her.

"Caw!" A crow flew across the road and brought her attention to the intersection a few yards ahead.

There was a white van sitting at the stop sign, just on the other side of the road. She froze.

The windows were tinted. A bit of a foggy morning dew covered the hood. The windshield wipers went across the black tinted windshield—an uneasy and painfully slow flip... flop... flip... flop....

Was that the same van? Had the two shadowy people inside it seen her? She tried to slide behind the nearest light pole, waiting for the van to complete the stop at the stop sign and go away. But the van did not move. It sat idling, a puff of smoke clouding out the back.

Lilac turned around and ran in a panic. As she did, she heard the screech of the van's tires as it took off.

She wanted to drop the bags of cat kibble and noodles to pick up speed, but she had come so far for that kibble, and her cat was counting on her.

She turned into a narrow alleyway between two small apartment buildings. She ran as fast as she could and ducked into a hut where the apartments stored their garbage cans. With a bit of a clatter, she pulled herself and her bags into the hut and stayed as quiet as she could, although the sound of her breath and blood racing with fear felt loud enough to give away her whereabouts.

She sat for at least ten minutes or so, maybe more, the smell of garbage wafting thick around her. If they couldn't find her, they'd eventually give up, she thought. Or so she hoped. And she needed to rest for a minute and catch her breath, anyway.

When she heard the sounds of the neighborhood waking up around her, Lilac took it as a sign to leave. She gathered her things. She crossed her fingers and hoped that the van was long gone. As nonchalantly as she could, she slipped out of the garbage hut. Then she took off, her heart pounding with every step, the plastic bag of noodles and canned fish swaying awkwardly at her side as she ran.

She went an extra block out of the way, to the far outskirts of the neighborhood bordering the edge of town, and found the long road that passed behind the back of Skully Manor.

It was eerily quiet again, and Lilac listened for sounds of something that would give her a sense of safety—maybe a family with kids, or at least a happy flock of birds, or a mom with a baby. But she heard the faint bark of dogs. Loud, angry sounding dogs in the distance.

She quickened the pace of her steps, jostling her kibble and glancing behind her.

Bark, bark, bark. She heard again, this time maybe even a little closer than before. Probably someone out walking their dogs on leashes, she thought to calm herself down. Lilac Skully was a cat person. She wanted to run faster but began to feel out of breath.

Bark bark bark, she heard again, louder still. A car engine revved behind her and startled her so badly, she gasped and tripped on a scraggly sidewalk. Her body fell forward, and Lilac was barely able to catch herself in time to avoid smashing her face on the concrete. A small red car whizzed by. She breathed a sigh of relief and caught her balance.

Lilac's pace quickened as she steadied her nerves.

Bark, bark, bark, she heard, and she felt her heart jump into her throat again. She began to get a terrible feeling that the dogs were chasing her.

She glanced over her shoulder and caught a glimpse of three gigantic, gleaming black dogs galloping in formation, merely yards away. Her body jolted into high gear and took off faster, a panicked gasp in her breath.

Bark, bark, bark. The sound tore through her ears. She didn't have to turn around to know that they were steps away. She couldn't outrun the dogs, and she knew she was running out of time before her legs collapsed, and she wouldn't be able to stay out of their reach.

Bark, bark, bark. She heard the scraping of their toenails against the sidewalk behind her. She saw a building across the street with a fire escape ladder. If she could get to that ladder and climb it, maybe they wouldn't be able to follow her.

Just then, a terrible, raspy voice called out in front of Lilac and sent chills down her spine. Peering out from behind a tree, something horrifying cried out. It was a hunched figure in a ratty, tattered cloak, yelling wildly and gristly, in a dark message of doom and despair. Lilac did not want to hear the words, but she couldn't help it.

"Hellhounds!" The cloaked figure hissed to Lilac. "Hellhounds!"

Lilac screamed and darted back and to the side, only shortening the distance between herself and the dogs. She saw a glimpse of glowing red in their eyes and let out another terrible scream. Her body pushed into a panic and she made an involuntary move to save herself.

She darted in between two parked cars, jumped up onto the bumper of one, off the hood of the other, and leaped across the street, her legs pushing with their last bit of adrenaline.

Screeeeeeeeeeech. A wide-ended, wood-paneled station wagon slammed on its brakes as Lilac flung herself across the street.

Lilac saw herself flying through the air as if she were tumbling in slow motion. Everything looked kind of funny, upside down and twirling around in circles. She smiled a bit and then landed with a thud on the road.

4.

BAD NEWS FOR MISS SKULLY

"**W**ha'dya doin' you dumb kid?" She heard an angry man yell.

Then, the sound of footsteps. She sat up. There was cat kibble strewn around her, and she was holding a busted-up bag in her hand. She picked up her plastic bag of noodles and cans of tuna, which had sort of cushioned her fall while crunching underneath her when she landed.

"You ran right out in front of my car, you... idiot!" The man yelled at her.

"The... d...d... death dogs!" Lilac tried to explain, "Hellhounds! Chasing me!" she said in shock, but then realized it was of no use explaining to him. She didn't hesitate any longer.

She got herself up and ran, as fast as she could. She glanced behind for any sign of the dogs, but they were gone. Just then the hooded figure popped out in front of her again, waving a warped, warty finger and screeching dramatically, this time something else.

"Run, girl! Run!" the cloaked figure yelled. "Run!"

Lilac's feet pounded the sidewalk. Her lungs and throat felt like sandpaper, but she didn't stop or slow down. She tried to listen for the dogs but could only hear the sound of her gasping breath. Her legs struggled to push her forward towards home and safety, despite the feeling of exhaustion and shock.

When she got in sight of Skully Manor, a few hundred yards in the distance, she broke out into a cold sweat. She finally flung herself through the garden gate, and its latch clanged loudly as it bounced closed behind her. Lilac ran around the back of the house and to the kitchen door.

Fumbling wildly for the key in her pocket, she noticed her knuckles, knees, and elbows were scraped up and bleeding badly at various points. She hadn't felt it before, but she certainly did now. Hot pangs of searing pain lit up in each spot as the blood began to seep through her sleeves, corduroys, and tights. Suddenly, everything hurt.

"You're ok," she whispered to herself as she tried to steady her stinging hands and fingers enough to unlock the door. "You made it, Lilac," she said. "You're home."

She got the key in and twisted it. The door fell open, and Lilac fell with it.

She locked all of the locks and laid down on her stomach, sprawled on the floor of the kitchen. The torn, empty bag of kibble was still clutched in one hand, the bag of crunched up noodles and cans of fish shaking from the tremble of her body in the other.

"Aaaaah!" She let out an exasperated wail.

"Mrow?" Casper asked, hopeful for food.

"I got your food," she told him as calmly as she could, "and I'm gonna feed you now," she said, extending a shaking hand out to pet him a few times and steady herself. "One of the bags of kibble didn't make it. But there should still be enough for a while. I'm glad I bought two."

She got up and opened a can of mackerel. Her hands were trembling and the fork clinked against the side of the bowl.

"You're going to have to start eating some kibble," she told him quietly as she set down his fish. "But today you can have mackerel, to make up for running out of food last night." She nodded to herself. That seemed fair.

Casper didn't look up from his food, and concentrated solely on the generous portion she'd given him.

"I know this has been hard on you," she told her cat, "with my father gone and everything." She took a deep breath and put the teakettle on the stove. She sat down at the kitchen counter and rested her head into her folded arms. Her scratches and scrapes were hurting a bit more every moment, it seemed.

Bram's voice called to her from behind the doorway to the dining hall.

"I'm sorry to disturb you, Miss Skully,"

"Come in, Bram," said Lilac, sitting up again.

"It's more bad news, Miss Skully,"

Lilac's brain began to think of all the terrible things that he might tell her. She had thought of three or four things before she got impatient.

"Just tell me, Bram!" Lilac pleaded.

"While you were out," he continued delicately, looking for the right words, "the house was broken into again, I'm afraid."

Lilac sat blankly, then shrugged and laughed a little bit, covering her face with her hands. Considering she'd just been chased by death dogs or hellhounds or whatever they were and had crashed into a large station wagon driven by an angry man—the bad news that the house was robbed for a third time in three days didn't seem *that* bad. Or did it?

"Well, I'm not surprised. What happened?" she asked Bram.

"The van pulled down the driveway shortly after you left, Miss Skully. Milly and I disappeared, and of course, we feared they were here to kidnap us. But we were relieved to find that wasn't the case, not this time."

Bram shuddered.

"So what did they do?" Lilac asked.

"They came in through the basement door and took something from the laboratory. I believe it was the second half of your father's paranormal communication equipment. They left in minutes. As quickly as they had come in, really."

"I see," Lilac said and thought for a moment.

The kettle whistled. Lilac hopped off her stool and got out a tea bag, a cup, a bowl, and a spoon. She emptied an utterly crushed bag of noodles into the bowl, along with the contents of the salty, silver flavor packet. She put the tea bag in the cup. She poured hot water into both the cup and the bowl and turned back to Bram.

"I expected something worse," she told him as she stirred the small bits of broken noodle and the contents of the flavor packet together with the hot water.

She took a bite. It was boiling, but it tasted good. She fanned her mouth a bit. Other than cups of tea, it was the first time she'd had hot food for several weeks. She pulled her legs up to her body and curled up cozily on the top of the stool. She didn't say anything. She fanned the top of the noodles and took a few more careful, steaming hot bites.

Bram waited for her further response but did not get one.

Lilac's soup had cooled enough to where she could drink the broth, and she began slurping it. It was like salty hot tea. Delicious, she thought.

"Well, aren't you concerned?" Bram asked.

Lilac shrugged, and sipped more soup.

"It's the third time they've broken in. And they came in while I was gone. They must have seen me leave." She slurped again, realizing the crushed noodles might turn out to be a good thing because she could gulp them easier out of the side of the bowl without using a spoon or fork.

"So they didn't try to capture you and Milly?" Lilac asked.

"No, they didn't." Bram said.

"I'd say it could be worse then," Lilac said with a nod. "If they wanted me, I'm here all the time, and so are both of you."

Bram couldn't think of much to argue with that, and did not respond.

Lilac finished off the rest of her soup. She turned back to Bram.

"Maybe we broke all of their ghost-hunting equipment, so they don't have any orbs left to trap you guys in." Lilac pondered. "Or maybe they're afraid of me now, because I sliced one of them with a sword. Remember?" She stood up and left the kitchen without *r* word.

Her scrapes and scratches were throbbing rhythmically, but she went downstairs to the cellar. The house was in her care. If it had been broken into again, she needed to assess the situation.

She saw immediately that her efforts to shore up the broken door had failed. Other than that, nothing looked different. She went into her father's lab and confirmed what Bram had suspected. They'd taken the second half of her father's paranormal communication equipment.

Lilac sighed. She'd really screwed that one up—twice. She should have just left the equipment hidden under the kitchen floor and never taken it back out. All of the effort she had put into keeping it out of their hands the night before had been wasted. She'd been a fool.

"Hi Lilac," Milly said from behind her. "They broke in again while you were gone!"

"Bram told me," Lilac said, still feeling utterly awful for her foolishness. "So stupid," Lilac sighed. "I should'a just left it hidden."

"You were just trying to help," Milly said. "You were trying to contact your father and find Archie. You meant well."

"Yeah, I tried to do something to help," Lilac said, "but, I failed."

"Well, you can't give up now," Milly told her.

Lilac laughed a little, "I can't?"

"No," Milly smiled back. "Not yet."

"Okay." Lilac said with a nod. "And I still have a clue to follow, I guess. The address at Gremory. They don't seem to have any problem breaking into my house, so why should I be concerned about breaking into theirs?"

"That's the spirit!" Milly said. "I believe in you, Lilac. We all do."

Lilac smiled, shyly.

"Thanks. Well, I'll see you soon, Milly, I've got to go wash out these scrapes and things." She pulled up her sleeve and revealed a jarring red abrasion on her pale elbow.

"Oh!" Milly started back horrified as she looked at the road rash that Lilac held up. "I'd almost forgotten what it's like to have terribly delicate flesh and feel physical pain," she added quietly. "That looks absolutely horrible, Lilac!" Milly then wailed.

"It's not... that bad...?" Lilac said in sort of a question, not quite sure herself.

Lilac headed toward the stairs. Her legs didn't want to cooperate. The morning's walk and events had already taken a toll on her nerves and body, her last bit of energy spent long ago while being chased by the hellhounds. The scrapes on her arms, elbows, and knees began to sting and draw attention to themselves more urgently.

She went through the foyer and upstairs to the second-floor bathroom, eventually climbing into a tub of hot, steaming, soapy water.

5.

"Sorrow for the Lost Lenore"

The wounds stung as she sat into the bath. She expected they would, but still, she winced. Tears fell down her cheeks as the pain began to fade. She stared up at the cracked plaster on the pale yellow ceiling, her light hair and skin blending in almost perfectly with the murky layer of soap on the top of the bath water. Only her round, wide eyes stood out.

She began to process the morning's events and wondered exactly what had happened. Had she been hit by that station wagon? Narrowly missed? She'd rolled over it for sure. She knew that much. Had she jumped on top of it?

What about that frightening, raspy hooded figure, yelling about hellhounds? Was there really such a thing? Or were they just big, scary dogs? The screeching voice echoed in her head, along with the terrible barking of the dogs. And did the dogs really have glowing red eyes? Perhaps it was just the morning sun gleaming off of their pupils? Had that been the same white van at the intersection? Did they see her? And were they coming back? And when?

Her journey out into the world that morning had been harrowing. She didn't want to leave the house ever again. But she couldn't stay there alone much longer, either. She and the ghosts were in danger. And she knew she'd have to leave sooner or later if she was going to find her father.

She set a washcloth gently over the spots of road rash, careful not to cause herself any more anguish. The hot bath calmed her down considerably. When she remembered that she still hadn't read what was in her mother's notebook, she got out of the bath right away.

She made another cup of tea in the kitchen and took it upstairs to her room. She closed her door, even though the ghosts could float right through the walls if they wanted, it felt cozier that way. She sat on the bed and opened the notebook. She closed it again. She read her mother's name in her mother's handwriting over and over.

Lenore Skully.

She was afraid it would be a disappointment, not as magical as she hoped it might be. She drank some more tea, then considered taking a nap or doing something else before reading what was inside. She opened the notebook again, and read the first page.

June 11,

Exciting developments today in the lab! Marvin's been struggling with his new electromagnetic frequency detector for a couple of weeks now. He insisted I not look at it, even though I've hinted several times that I thought I could fix it. But today he left it out on the workbench, and I had it working by the time he was back with tea! Ha!

I had a good laugh and a tease at him, and eventually, he laughed, too. He admitted he was lucky to have me as his research partner, let alone his wife!

I think that's the wonderful thing about Marvin, he's not too serious and keeps it light, even when we're working on scientific research together. Maybe that's the secret to our success in this field.

Oh! And on that subject... I didn't mention yet that the Paranormal Times is writing an article on us for the Fall Quarterly! Exciting. Well, Marvin suggested we go to Dom Giulio's for dinner to celebrate the article, and then we've got permission to do an investigation tonight, and bring the new and improved EMF detector (that I fixed!) to the old roadhouse. Excited to see what we can pick up in that location with this new equipment.

Lilac paused, a slight smile on her lips. Marvin was her father. But the way her mother described him, a fun person who kept things light? That didn't seem like her father at all. Lilac thought that was a little funny, but then she felt sad that he'd changed so much, and seemingly not for the better.

But still, it was a welcome relief, and her mother's writing had lifted her mood just a bit. The fear that it would be disappointing or depressing faded. The expectation that it would be earth-shattering in some way also left, which was sort of nice, because now Lilac had a reasonable amount of happiness that she could return to. And she looked forward to exploring each page.

Her mother *did* seem nice. Milly had said that, but she thought Milly was just making it up to make her feel better. However, she could already tell from reading just one entry that her mother was warm and kind and pleasant and fun to be with. Lilac smiled, even though it just didn't seem fair. She closed the notebook and set it down on the bedside table.

Thinking about her parents investigating ghosts together long ago, before she was born, made her happy, even though it was also making her sad. Her mother's enthusiasm for the subject was comforting to Lilac. She wanted to write an article and go out to a restaurant, too. She wondered if Dom Giulio's was still open. She imagined eating a huge plate of spaghetti and meatballs with garlic bread and parmesan cheese. She was tired. She had barely slept the night before. She made sure her bedroom door was locked, shut out the lights, and fell asleep for a nap.

When Lilac awoke, it was later than she had expected. The sun was already starting to fade in the darkening autumn sky. When she looked at the clock, she was shocked to see it was already 3:45 in the afternoon.

She tried to shake off the extra sleepy grogginess that settles in when you oversleep in the middle of the day. She sat on the edge of the bed and nodded once to herself, decidedly. It was time to start getting a plan ready. Yes, it was overwhelming. And no, she didn't really know what she was doing or where she was going. And it made her feel sick with dread to think about leaving the manor again. But she had to start somewhere and follow the one clue she had—the address of Black, Black, and Gremory.

Lilac tucked her mother's folder into the drawer of her bedside table and read through the other papers and strange letters she'd collected. She didn't quite understand what it all meant, but she was pretty sure her father was in trouble and Forsyth Gremory was trying to get something from him—some information or invention. They had offered him a job at their facility several times, and from what she could tell, he had declined. And they were threatening not just him, but his family. She reread the most recent letter from Mr. Gremory, dated just a year ago. When she got to the part that worried her, she read it out loud.

"If you are unwilling to cooperate, we will be forced to take drastic measures which, may not be in the best interest of you and your family—living and dead."

Lilac gulped and felt cold. His family, living and dead. His only living family was her. So that alone was enough for concern. But his dead family? How could Forsyth Gremory threaten his family that was already dead? What did that mean? All of his family was dead at this point except for her. Even his dead relatives were few. He was an only child, and his father had been, too. Lilac suddenly realized she knew nothing about her mother's family. Not even her mother's maiden name. The only relatives she'd ever heard about were her father's, The Skullys.

She looked at the dates of the letters, and the tone seemed to darken with each one. She supposed the specifics of it didn't matter much at that point. It didn't change what she needed to do. Her only clue was the same.

"11011 Old Cemetery Road, Steamville," she read off of the letterhead. She knew where that road was at least. It started just behind Skully Manor but a block or two away, at the old cemetery, and then it ran several miles along the eastern edge of town. It was a long, straight road that bordered the woods. Lilac suspected that the address "11011" was miles down the road, although she wasn't sure how far.

She took her papers with her and went downstairs to the library to try and find a map. She turned the lights on and was taken aback. She hadn't been in the library since she'd sliced the intruder's leg with her sword. The panic of this incident refreshed itself as Lilac looked around in horror. A massive quantity of thick dried blood had soaked into the carpet and squirted out over the ornate antique furnishings. It was a dark blemish on the once beautiful library, and a stark reminder of what she had done, and how deep into this she already was. Looking at all the blood, she was fairly certain she'd killed the man, and that she would go down in history as a notorious murderer.

Although she felt ice cold and utterly horrified, she composed herself and hopped lightly through the room, carefully avoiding any swaths of dried blood, as if it mattered.

She knew her father kept a drawer of maps in the

library and hoped she could find one of Steamville to reference. There was indeed a map of the town, and although it was over forty years old, it would have to do. The map featured historical points of interest in the town of Steamville, and Lilac smiled to see Skully Manor called out, with a little illustration and everything.

"Skully Manor!" She read off of the map with delight. "Historic Point of Interest, and The Most Haunted House in Steamville." Her excitement faded. She wondered if that was still true now that Mr. Fright and Archie were gone. Even the elusive Blue Lady was gone. There were only two out of five ghosts left at Skully Manor. A chill rushed through her. She went back to the map.

The location of her own house on the map gave her easy bearings to see where she was and where she wanted to go. She found Cemetery Road, which she knew had been changed to "Old Cemetery Road" sometime in the past forty years since the map had been printed, and a newer cemetery was put in on the other side of town. And since the map was so old, it only went to the 8000's of Cemetery Road. She needed to go to further, to 11011, but at least she had the general direction. She folded the map back up and walked to the library door. As she turned off the lights, Lilac wished the dried blood and mess inside would disappear if she forgot about it long enough, but she knew it wouldn't. She shut the door behind her.

Lilac took her map back into the kitchen and set it on the counter. She had a sinking feeling that what she was about to do was incredibly foolish. She didn't even know if her father was at that address. And if he were, she'd have to travel over six miles round trip on foot—following an outdated map—without getting noticed or kidnapped or killed. It seemed like the worst clue ever, certainly not the caliber of something Nancy Drew would find.

The kettle whistled, and she fixed another cup of tea and a bowl of crushed instant noodles. She sipped the soupy broth and stared down at the map for a few moments.

Then, Lilac saw a faint reverberation in the liquid of her tea and soup, rumbling out from the center in ripples. Her cup began to rattle in the saucer. The lights flickered and lamps started to sway. There was an unsettling roar that got louder and louder. The wooden walls of Skully Manor began to shake, tremble and creak.

"What's happening?!" Lilac said out loud to no one, sliding off of her stool and steadying her feet on the floor.

Behind the curtain, Lilac saw the silhouette of a massive creature screech to a halt amongst the weeds and thistles—just outside the kitchen door.

6.

THE CARRIAGE OF LOST SOULS

The rumbling stopped. Bram burst through the kitchen wall.

"Neigh!" Lilac heard a horse and the sound of impatient hooves stomping on the ground outside.

"It can't be!" Bram approached the window and clutched one hand to his chest. Lilac ran after him and pushed aside the curtains to peek out.

A horse-drawn carriage had pulled up behind Skully Manor. Lilac gasped.

It was unlike any carriage she'd seen at the museum or in the historical parade. It was a ghost carriage.

She could see a million tiny cracks in the bone-white enamel of the carriage, as if the whole thing might burst into dust at any second. The massive wood-spoked wheels had road-worn spikes coming out of the hubs. The carriage walls were deeply curved, with leaded glass windows on either side of the narrow door. The shapes and symbols etched on the glass were things that Lilac had never seen before. There were angels with strange musical instruments and mythical animals who danced to their songs. She saw a mystical, magical alphabet that must have been in another language from another time because Lilac could not read the letters. There were dark, elaborately pleated curtains that covered the windows. The carriage had an eerie translucent blue glow and it faded in and out of form so slowly that if she blinked hard enough, Lilac thought it might disappear.

And pulling the carriage was a magnificent, glimmering ghost horse. It was the biggest horse she'd ever seen. The top of his back must have been over eight feet tall, and his head towered even higher. The horse's mane, tail, and coat were an ethereal glowing blonde-white. Lilac smiled, because the horse's hair had the same wild, stark look as her own, and she'd never seen anyone else with hair just like hers.

"What... is that?" Lilac whispered to Bram.

"It's the Carriage..." Bram said. "The Carriage of Lost Souls..." he added and paused again. "It brings the dead home to haunt." Bram said in the slightest, breathless whisper. "Oh dear, it's been a while..."

Bram didn't look at Lilac. Instead he stared straight ahead, his eyes fixed out the window on the carriage. He drifted into thought and then spoke again. "I wonder who died!" he said, and clasped his hand over his mouth.

Lilac felt a cold rush. If the carriage meant someone died, then... who died? She felt sick. It had to be her father. He was the only other living person who lived there. Who else could it be?

Just then, a tall, thin man with a top hat hopped down from the driver's seat.

"Easy now, Titan!" the man called to the massive ghost horse.

"Lilac, open the door," Bram said.

She hesitated for a moment, not wanting to deal with what was on the other side, especially if it had to do with the death of her father. But she opened the door as Bram had asked.

"Stewart!" Bram called out to the carriage driver.

Stewart smiled and tilted his glasses. "Bram!" he replied with a smile.

The coachman was wearing a dark coat with seven buttons up the front. It fell just above his knees, with a few inches of cream-colored pants visible before they tucked into his tall, cuffed boots.

Stewart stepped into the house, and the two ghosts embraced briefly in a faint cloud of dust. The unfamiliar scent of Stewart's ghost filled up the kitchen. It was similar to the sweet and strange scent of the ghosts of Skully Manor, but there was also a horsey, hay-like aroma to it, like an ancient stable mixed with a bit of an oily, greasy tinge. Lilac tilted her head to the side and stared at him, bewildered.

"Well, I'm, uh, I'm sorry I haven't been back by to see you since, uh," Stewart said and stopped mid-sentence.

"I understand," Bram said seriously, and reached out to clasp Stewart on the shoulder.

"I just want you to know," Stewart said to Bram, "I'm sorry, and I really miss you as a friend, despite everything." He paused. "I just want you to know that."

Bram was quiet for a moment, and Lilac wondered what "despite everything" meant between the two of them but she knew better than to pry.

"All is forgiven," Bram finally said, and gave a nod to the carriage driver.

"Well! Let's take care of business then," Stewart said. "I've got a young man that's anxious to return home." Stewart went back to the carriage door and opened it.

It was Archie. His unmistakable apparition in a pale blue sailor suit and cap flung out of the carriage. He gasped and grabbed for the doorway.

"Archie!" Lilac cried out.

"Oh, thank heavens!" Bram said, and let out a sigh of relief.

A wave of joy washed over Lilac, and she jumped up and down at the sight of the little ghost. The color returned to her face. She was so happy to see Archie, and so relieved that the ghost of her father was not in the carriage. He was still alive. Unless he was dead and just wasn't coming back to haunt as a ghost, she thought. She still wondered how that worked.

"I'm home!" the spirit of the little boy yelled with glee. "Lilac!" He saw Lilac and looked at her with wide eyes. "They've got your father!" he gasped.

Archie flew through the kitchen wall in a glowing cloud of blue dust, and called his sister's name, "Milly! Oh! Milly!"

"I found the little guy lost on the Old Ghost's Road," Stewart explained to Bram. "Bound to get himself captured again. Surprised they didn't come after him, with all that's going on out there."

"What?" Lilac interjected. "What's going on? Out where?" she asked.

"Ghostnappings! Haven't you heard?" Stewart said to her, the jovial, friendly tones from just a few moments ago entirely gone. "The dead've gone missing," he added slowly, his black, swirling eyes fixed on her.

Lilac already knew that, but the way he said it made her feel dark and awful, so she didn't respond.

"Why two ghosts were taken from right here in this very house and garden, don't you know?" he continued, as if she were oblivious to the obvious.

"Y... yes, I know that, and my father, too!" she got the guts to say back to him. "I'm pretty sure he was kidnapped." She folded her arms.

"Well that's a terrible thing to hear," Stewart said, shaking his head. "There's nothing good about what's been happening at that Gremory place."

"Gremory?" Lilac's ears perked up when she heard the name, but she also shuddered as a draft blew through the manor.

"Yeah that's where I picked up your boy Archie," he added, "It's dangerous on that old road!" He got a serious look on his face, and motioned to his carriage. "Speaking of, I've got to let Titan rest up before the midnight cemetery run." He tipped his hat. "Bram, my old friend," he clasped Bram's shoulder, and Bram reached back. "I'll be back to visit soon."

"Don't be a stranger," Bram said to him. "What's past is past," he added.

Stewart got a funny look in his eyes and nodded at Bram.

"Wait!" Lilac cried out to the coachman. "Can you take me back there? To Black, Black, and Gremory?"

"Carry a living girl?" Stewart laughed in disbelief. "In the Carriage of Lost Souls?!" He chuckled.

"I'm not an ordinary... 'living,'" Lilac tried to explain herself. "As you can see," she motioned to Bram next to her, "I prefer the company of ghosts, and I consider them my friends." She tried to look as friendly as possible, yet remain serious, and not too cute or helpless. She furrowed her brow just a little.

"I don't think so," Stewart said. "It's my sworn duty to pick up any souls I find wandering the Old Ghost's Road—lost ones, dead ones, evil ones, all kinds. Why, I get demons and witches and walkers and strange creatures of all sorts, things I can't explain." He shook his head. "Things you wouldn't want to know," he added. "A lot of dangers out there to the living *and* the dead, Miss, a lot of them in my carriage," he said, shaking his head.

"I'm not just... some little girl!" she said. "I'm a Skully! And besides, I'm... a lost soul—sort of—and I'm here alone and in danger anyway, and they broke into my house three times." She nodded, holding up three fingers, and continued. "I'm going there to get my father anyway," she folded her arms. "By myself. A ride would just make it easier, so I know I'm at the right place."

Stewart looked at Bram. Bram gave him a minuscule nod of approval, not more than a flinch, and Stewart's eyes narrowed, the expression on his face was dark and suspicious.

"If you can climb aboard without falling through the floor like a ninny, you can ride." He motioned to the carriage step.

Lilac hesitated. Titan stamped and neighed impatiently.

Lilac walked to the carriage and lifted her foot. Half

expecting to plop right through the translucent form of the ghost carriage, she shifted her weight and stepped gingerly. But the carriage felt solid under her feet. She smiled and stood right up. At most, she thought it would be soft like a cloud, but it felt as substantial as if it belonged to the living.

Stewart nodded and shrugged. "The route along the Old Ghost's Road leaves at midnight," he said, and Lilac stepped down.

"The Old *Cemetery* Road?" Lilac confirmed, not sure about the Old Ghost's Road, but thinking he meant the same.

"One and the same, Miss," Stewart said back to her seriously. "Depends what side you're on," he added, raising his eyebrows.

Lilac's eyes widened.

"Be at the roadhouse before midnight, no later." He wagged a spectral finger at her in a blur. "Titan keeps a tight schedule and won't be waiting." He nodded to Bram and looked back at Lilac.

Lilac knew where the old roadhouse was. Everyone did. It was curious that her mother's notebook had just referenced it, too. How very strange, she thought.

The old roadhouse was close to Skully Manor, just on the other side of the cemetery behind the house, on the edge of the woods. The roadhouse also happened to be the start of the Old Cemetery Road, or the Old Ghost's Road as it was called, depending on if you were living or dead.

Lilac nodded slowly to Stewart. "I'll be there," she told him in her most calm and confident voice.

"And you ride at your own risk, little girl," he said. "I mean that," he said directly to Bram.

Bram nodded once, his hands clasped behind his back.

Stewart tipped his top hat to him and turned back towards his carriage, nimbly floating up to his seat and cracking the reins with a ghastly yell. Titan reared up, and with thunderous hooves, the Carriage of Lost Souls pulled away from Skully Manor, and out towards the Old Ghost's Road.

7.

The Haunted Roadhouse

Bram smiled, somewhat sadly from what Lilac could tell, and he seemed content not to talk or have any further questions asked about the conversation with Stewart.

"Thanks, Bram," Lilac said as she hurried out of the kitchen. "I've got to talk to Archie about my father and get ready for tonight."

He did not reply.

She found Milly and Archie in her bedroom. Archie was back in his favorite rocking chair in the corner, rocking slowly back and forth as he liked to do. Milly jumped off the bed and swooshed towards Lilac.

"Lilac! Archie came back! You were right!" Milly cried with happy tears.

"Lilac!" Archie called to her from the rocking chair. "I saw your father!"

A creepy feeling crawled through Lilac's bones.

"Where is he?" she asked Archie, "How do I get to him? How did you escape?"

"Oh! It was horrible!" Archie's eyes were wide with

excitement and terror, as Milly and Lilac hung on every word he said.

"They have a whole bunch of ghosts trapped in a big room, and each ghost is in a cylinder, kinda like the orbs, but kinda different. And I saw the Blue Lady there too! And lots of others! I saw 'em," Archie said gravely.

"Your father's in one of the laboratory rooms. He's working on some of the equipment with the men. And there were lots of other ghosts there, all trapped!" He began to tremble. "So many of them!" he added in a loud whisper.

"And then they transferred me into a cylinder next to the Blue Lady. I couldn't believe it when I saw her, but it was really her." He nodded intently, seriously. "I know it was! And she saw me too! And then I felt something funny, like a whoosh of air, and I realized something was wrong with my cylinder, and I could escape! But they had that same electricity going through the walls of the building, like in the orb, so I found my way out by floating through this little tunnel with warm air. But then I was lost in the woods! I didn't know what to do or where to go..." Archie trailed off in his memory.

As she listened to his stories, Lilac began to wonder if she was getting herself in too deep, and felt an eerie, gnawing pang of doubt. Was hitching a ride in the ghost carriage an incredibly foolish thing to do? Perhaps. But she had to do something. And this was her chance to get a ride straight to Black, Black and Gremory. It wasn't a coincidence. Things were lining up. All she had to do was get herself into the Carriage of Lost Souls before midnight.

"Well, it's seven o'clock," she announced as she looked at the clock. "I've got five hours till I need to be at the roadhouse."

She filled her backpack with some jars of tap water, crackers, rope, a hammer, wire cutters, two cans of dolmas, and any other tools she could find. A pair of scissors. Knitting needles. A few pieces of the papier-mâché fruit she had used to stuff up the ghost-trapping orb when the men had broken into her house. It had come in handy once, and it might again, she reasoned.

She wished she could bring her sword but thought it might look suspicious if she brought it in the ghost carriage. Besides, she didn't have a proper sheath to carry it safely, so she left it hidden under the floorboards of the kitchen. She packed up for about an hour, till she couldn't think of anything else to pack. She wondered if she had enough food and water, but she didn't know how long she'd be gone. She started to worry that it might be a while.

"Hopefully not *too* long," she said. "Maybe I can even get Father out tonight."

She made some tea and another package of noodles. She ate some peanut butter off of a spoon, knowing she had to keep her strength up for the night's journey. After her snack, she remembered she hadn't packed her flashlight, so she dashed off to get that, and then rummaged through the kitchen junk drawer and her father's lab till she found a couple extra sets of batteries.

She looked at the clock. "8:15," she said. "three hours and forty-five minutes."

She tried to think what she might do for three hours and forty-five minutes to pass the time. She went to her closet and found a sensible outfit for an undercover mission. She wore her thickest woolen tights with brown corduroy pants over them and black and white striped socks underneath. She put on her warmest purple velvet long-sleeved dress, rubber soled lace-up boots, and a heavy black wool coat with a hood. The hood draped over her head dramatically and covered her distinctive bright, blonde hair. She hoped to blend into the shadows of the night and keep her hair from shining in the moonlight, at least.

She put on her wristwatch. It said 8:30.

"Three and a half hours," she said. "It'll take me at least ten minutes to walk there, and I don't want to be late. So I'll leave here at 11:30..." she recalculated, "three hours."

She tried to think of something to do for three hours. She went to talk to Bram. Lilac was worried that if she left, the ghosts would be defenseless if the ghost hunters came back. At least she could help protect them if she stayed at the manor. Maybe she shouldn't leave.

But Bram reassured her that they'd planned some better defense tactics using his possession skills, Archie's abilities as a poltergeist, and Milly's talents with electrical currents. And he agreed that Lilac had to do something to try and find her father. Yet Lilac felt a cold, unsettling feeling about everything.

She left a large bowl of kibble for Casper and instructed Archie to pour more kibble if it ran out before she got back.

"But it shouldn't," she said, "I think I'll be back soon. Maybe even by morning," she told the ghosts of Skully Manor, confidently.

She set her alarm clock and tried to sleep, but she could not. She tried to read her *Nancy Drew* book to get in the investigative spirit but found the words jumping around on the page.

She must have dozed off because the blaring alarm bell jolted her awake at 11:30 p.m. She jumped out of bed, her body in a deep sleep, and shook off the confusion and grogginess. She didn't have time for tea. She couldn't be late.

Dressed with her boots on, she put on her backpack and went downstairs. Lilac took the skeleton key out of the kitchen drawer. She slipped out the back door, locked it behind her, and buttoned the key safely in the pocket of her corduroy pants. She held her breath and stepped out into the night.

The air was crisp and silent. Lilac heard the crunch of the gravel and weeds under her feet as she tried to walk as quietly as possible.

She pulled her hood up and emerged from the shadows of Skully Manor. She opened the back garden gate.

Creeeeeeeeak went the hinge on the rusty old gate. Lilac's eyes widened as she paused, then listened to see if anyone might have heard or seen her. Silence. She stepped through the gate and onto the craggy, jagged bit of sidewalk that had been pushed up by the tree roots beneath. As quietly as she could, she walked down the road towards the old cemetery. It was just two large vacant lots from Skully Manor, and the roadhouse was on the other side. There was a path through the middle of the graveyard, but she dared not take it. She went around the block on the sidewalk, tucked in from the street, and stayed in the shadows of the trees. The moon was bright above her, which made it harder for her to hide, but a little less scary since she was not in total darkness.

Midnight was not as frightening as she had imagined. There was the faint glow from television sets in the windows of neighboring houses. She noticed a few cars and other signs of life. People that might hear her scream, she thought, if something were to happen.

Lilac quickened her pace. She looked behind her and could see the silhouette of Skully Manor. It looked crooked, as if it was leaning towards her, reaching out for her, like it didn't want her to go, like it was calling her back. She turned away and kept walking. Under a grove of twisted, ancient oak trees up ahead, just on the other side of the cemetery, was the old roadhouse.

Lilac felt a sense of doom fall to the pit of her stomach when she saw her dark and shadowy destination. She'd driven by before and knew it didn't look like much from the outside, a dilapidated one-story rectangular building on the corner of the block, its windows boarded up long ago. The wood planks of the walls were never painted, so the decaying frame sagged and seemed to be sinking slowly back into the earth.

The roadhouse was known as one of the most haunted locations in town, and Lilac was headed straight for it. She tried to feel the same cavalier attitude of mystery and excitement that her mother had expressed when she wrote about investigating there. It didn't work. She still felt nervous and had to talk herself out of calling the whole thing off and going back home to hide.

As she got closer, Lilac began to wonder if the roadhouse was still there. The shadows of the trees obscured it completely. She couldn't make out the faintest hint of it in the darkness. As she kept walking, she thought she saw a familiar otherworldly flicker in the distance, only to have it fade out again. She stopped and squinted her eyes. She knew the roadhouse had to be there. But she couldn't see it. As if it were hidden somehow, she thought. She closed her eyes and then opened them again, just barely, and the shape of the old roadhouse slowly fuzzed into view.

She had no plan, other than to ride the carriage to Black, Black, and Gremory, and then rescue her father. She looked at her wristwatch. She was early for the midnight carriage. Maybe she could hide in the shadows a bit longer till she saw Titan and Stewart.

When she was satisfied that no one was watching, she scurried into the courtyard of the cemetery, where she could hide and get a better view. Lilac stopped short of the first row of graves and ducked down behind a fountain with nothing in it, other than the sludge that had collected since the last rain.

The roadhouse looked dark and empty. She didn't

see Stewart or Titan and the carriage or any other ghosts, anywhere. She crouched in the shadows and shifted her weight to get more comfortable.

Suddenly, a voice rang out from behind her in the graveyard. Lilac breathed in a seemingly endless breath. She tried to quiet herself to remain unseen from whatever horrible creature was behind her. She could not understand the words. It was another language, a raspy woman's voice reciting some sort of incantation. Worse, she realized she recognized the voice. It was the same terrible, scratchy, screaming figure from the other morning, the one that had been yelling about the hellhounds. Lilac didn't want to turn her head, but she did anyway, and she saw the same cloaked woman, hobbling amongst the graves, her arms outstretched.

Who was she? And why was she following her? What did she want? Lilac finally broke out of her crippling panic and ran. She darted out of the cemetery courtyard as quickly as she could, her body shaking as the instinct to flee charged through each cell. Her heart pounded, and she ran kitty-corner across the street, towards houses and people and civilization. She ducked into the darkness and tucked between two cars, then peered out to see if the cloaked figure was following. She gasped to catch her breath. That was it. She was going home. This was a bad idea.

Just then, she heard the thunderous pounding of Titan's hooves. It was no less impressive than when he'd first pulled up to her house. Lilac's eyes were transfixed on the beautiful horse as he trotted up to the roadhouse and tossed his mane wildly. Stewart climbed down from the carriage.

Lilac took a deep breath. She had to do it. This was her chance. She ran across the street.

"Hello Mr. Stewart," she tried to call to him as plainly as possible, without sounding terrified or childish or like it was out of the ordinary for a living girl to be hitching a ride in the Carriage of Lost Souls.

"Didn't think you'd show up, Skully," he said.

She shrugged. "I'm here," she looked at her watch, "early and ready to go," she added with a smile.

"The carriage leaves at midnight," he said to her bluntly. "You'd better stay close here, or better yet, get inside the carriage and don't leave." His eyebrows pinched, and he looked very stern. "This roadhouse is no place for the living, especially a little girl like you."

Lilac resented that, but she stayed put and did not argue. The roadhouse looked silent, dilapidated, and abandoned, just as it had been for years. But when Stewart swung the door open, Lilac was taken aback at what she saw.

Inside was a smoky, dusty, otherworldly sight. The

room was full of dozens of ghosts and ghouls, living it up with raucous laughter and conversation. A blue-green glow lit up the scene, and Lilac gazed at the clothing on the eerie men and women. They were dressed in styles from various eras, dresses and suits that looked like they were from the 1920s, military uniforms from foreign wars, and the kind of Victorian-style clothing that Lilac was used to seeing on the ghosts that haunted her house. She also noticed that some of the spirits were dressed in modern-day clothing and guessed that those were the souls who had died more recently. How sad, she thought.

Then a brawl broke out in the crowd. Lilac jumped back a step, covering the smile on her lips with her hand as she saw a man with half of a skeleton face punch another ghostly fellow in the jaw. One of the bartenders broke up the fight, and a wild-looking woman with a bottle of champagne shook it up and sprayed them all down.

Another ghost in full pirate regalia drank straight out of a bottle with one hand and held an ukulele with his other. The door slammed shut. The air around her fell back to the silence of the living world at midnight.

"Hi, Titan," she said gently as her attention fell on the white horse. She approached him cautiously.

"I'm... Lilac... Skully," she said, not sure what else

she should say to such a magnificent spirit. He whinnied and nudged his nose to meet her.

She reached her hand out, slowly, and though his figure was translucent and not really "there" like flesh and bone would be, Lilac could feel his steady form and presence. It was cool, a little bit prickly, yet soft and strong. She stroked his fuzzy nose a few times, and talked sweetly to him.

He nudged her again and snorted, then gently twisted his head this way and that a little bit for her to pet him in different spots. He clearly enjoyed the attention. Lilac marveled at the way his silvery white mane shook and shimmied with a spectral glow. She giggled. She had never pet a ghost horse before, and she'd never actually pet a living horse before, either.

The roadhouse door swung back open and Lilac darted into the shadows. It was Stewart.

"Load up, dead or alive," he said as he tipped his hat to Lilac, who he could see through the darkness. "I'm making the call to board."

"Hey Mr. Stewart?" Lilac asked. "How come the Gremory ghost-nappers don't come here since there are so many ghosts at the roadhouse?"

"Sorcery!" Stewart said with a maniacal laugh. "This place is cloaked. Honestly didn't think you'd find it." He shrugged. "All aboard!" he called out.

Lilac ran and gave Titan one more pet on the nose, and then hurried towards the carriage. She climbed the tall, steep steps and turned the handle of the door.

The heavy, thick, ghostly scent filled her nostrils. It took the breath out of her lungs and she paused. The inside of the carriage was dark, with dim flickering candles on four sconces, two at each end. Black velvet curtains covered the windows, and blood-red silk tassels hung beneath. The upholstery on the seats was tufted and buttoned, made of a strange, rough animal hide, still covered in coarse hair.

Lilac felt her body contract as she gasped for breath and struggled to move herself further inside. Her feet were frozen on the steps. It wasn't too late to turn around and run home. But then what? She'd promised herself. She was going to find her father.

She moved one foot forward, then another. She took two more steps, fought off the dizziness induced by the thick, fathomless atmosphere inside. And then Lilac took a seat inside the Carriage of Lost Souls.

8.

LITTLE WITCH

L ilac was the first passenger inside the carriage, so she moved all the way to the end of the row and sat in the corner. She made sure her hair was tucked into her hood and put her hands in her pockets. She looked down and straight ahead, and hoped to go unnoticed for the entire trip.

She was disappointed that the curtains were drawn and tied down tight, so she wouldn't be able to look out the window. She was pretty sure they were going all the way down the Old Cemetery Road, or the Old Ghost's Road as the dead called it, but she wasn't certain. She had hoped to look out and memorize the route so she could be sure to get back home, but she couldn't do that now.

There were footsteps and laughing voices outside, and the carriage rocked as someone stepped onto the platform. The door swung open again. The voices from outside rushed in with a spooky breeze. Lilac held her breath and tried not to look. But she did. There were two men and a woman. They appeared to be drunk. They were laughing and hanging on to each other and carrying on a bit, telling jokes that seemed to make no sense. Lilac thought they smelled like mothballs and gin, which was perfectly fine with her, as long as they kept to themselves.

Someone else stepped in, a woman who looked like she had been crying for days. She was holding a baby. Lilac noticed the woman was in modern clothes, and along with her sadness, she had a shocked, confused, and terrified sort of look about her. Like she'd never ridden in the carriage before, the way she hesitated and looked around, then sat down timidly, clutching her baby, and trying to remain unseen by the other passengers.

How very sad, Lilac thought, that the ghost baby had died so young, and the woman, too. She wondered if it was less sad that at least the mother and child had died together. Lilac was just a baby when her mother had died, and she'd never known her. She suddenly realized she wouldn't be there right now if she were dead. Or would she, she wondered? Her thoughts were interrupted as the last passenger stepped on board, and the door swung shut with a final latch.

Click.

Lilac's blood dropped. She went cold. The same

cloaked, mumbling, hobbling figure from the cemetery joined the crowd in the carriage. The figure sat across from Lilac on the opposite bench. Lilac wanted to get up and run, but she was frozen in terror. It was now the third time she'd encountered this same cloaked stranger. She was being followed. She knew it. And she was going to die, she realized. She wanted to stand up and run for her life, but she heard Stewart call out to Titan, and the wheels began to roll beneath the carriage floor. Lilac sat still and tried to keep breathing. There was no turning back.

Titan took off. The carriage began to rumble, jolt, and move faster and more wildly than Lilac had expected. Her hand darted out to try and hold on.

"Well! Who've we got here?" called out one of the drunk men in the carriage.

Lilac put her hand back into her pocket.

"You're not a ghost, are you?" the man said.

Lilac remained silent. The chatter in the carriage stopped.

"Since we're all riding together, we might as well get acquainted," he offered to the group.

Lilac said nothing and tried her hardest not to give off any feelings of fear. She noticed the cloaked figure and the young ghost woman with the baby weren't saying anything either, which made her feel slightly less rude for not responding.

"I'm Christopher Stefengraph, that's who I am, died at age twenty-seven. Fell down a well drinkin' and drowned."

His drunk companions burst out laughing at the tale of his death. Lilac and the two others remained silent and did not offer their introductions. Lilac hoped he would give up and stick with talking to his friends. He didn't.

"And we've got the newly dead here, haven't we?" he said as he nodded to the young woman with the baby. She huddled down further and looked as if she was going to cry even more. "Oh so sad, mum! But don't worry!" he added with a mocking tone of concern, "You'll get used to it, sooner or later!"

No one said anything.

He continued, "And I think that's the old Crone Hedge Witch Cerridwen Brimblecrom in the corner... isn't it? Jumping the hedge tonight, dear old witchy?"

The three drunk ghosts giggled and laughed. The cloaked figure gave a minuscule nod with her hooded head.

"See?" Christopher said. "Not all of us here are dead, then. No need to hide your true nature..."

The carriage fell deadly silent, even more than it

had been before.

"I'm talking to you, little bitty living one under the hood." His voice became far less playful.

"Leave her alone, Chris," the drunk ghost woman said, and hit him in the shoulder. "Can't you tell she's just a girl?"

"Well, what's a girl doing in the midnight Lost Soul's Carriage on the Ghost's Road? That's what I want to know," he said in a tone as if he thought he was Sherlock Holmes.

The last thing Lilac wanted was attention. And at this point, she felt like she had made it worse by not saying anything at all. But she stayed silent. The wheels rolled over the rough road. Titan's hooves hammered. Lilac's heart pounded. No one said anything else for a while.

"Off to find your dead mummy or something, are you, girl?" Christopher finally said and laughed callously. The drunk woman tried to shush him again. It was a low blow, and it hit Lilac hard.

"I'm a witch too!" Lilac yelled out suddenly, not knowing what she was doing or saying, but desperate to do something to defuse the situation. "And a witch's business is none of your business!" she added in the deepest, raspiest voice she could.

The old hedge witch in the corner laughed. It started

as a little chuckle, but then it seemed to grow almost out of control, like the whine and wheeze of a wailing engine, as if she couldn't stop herself from laughing.

Lilac turned red. The witch was laughing at her.

"Oooh!" Christopher laughed at her, too. In fact, she was pretty sure the entire carriage was, except for the poor ghost woman with the baby.

"A little witch, off alone to do very witchy things in the night." Christopher continued and waved his fingers in the air as he giggled. "Well, what could go wrong there, I wonder..." he scratched his chin. Lilac saw the drunk woman's satin high-heeled shoe kick him in the shin.

"What's your name, then?" he asked Lilac.

"Lily," said Lilac, and then not another word.

She felt a sense of relief as the driver called out the downtown stop, and the drunken crew looked like they were going to get off. The carriage slowed down, and the inquisitor and his two friends stood to leave. The woman with the baby got off. Then, the drunk woman and the other drunk man got off, but Christopher Stefengraph pulled back and called out to them.

"You know what, guys, I remember I've got somewhere else to go, I'll catch up with you later."

"Oh come on, Chris!" the lady pleaded with him.

"Just let him go, Esmeralda," the other man called to

the woman, taking her hand outside.

Christopher closed the carriage door, then sat in the first seat kitty-corner from Lilac. He stretched his long, creepy legs across to the next bench and blocked the exit.

Lilac felt sick with dread. Her vision blurred and her mind raced. She lowered her head. She didn't want to show fear, but she was terrified. She jumped up to flee in a panic, but was knocked back into the bench as the wheels began to roll and Titan quickly carried along his route.

Christopher chuckled and rubbed his chin, as if he were thinking.

"What stop are you off at, then, young witch Lily?" he asked Lilac.

"I said it's none of your business," she replied, as deeply and powerfully as she could from under her hood, yet her voice shook and stuttered.

Her answer silenced Christopher for a few moments, but she felt no better. If he was still in the carriage at her stop, he'd see exactly where she was going. And who was to stop him from following her at that point? She gulped. If she hadn't been doomed before, she certainly was now. It had only been an hour or so since she left the manor, and she was already being followed by a malevolent ghost and a witch. Just her luck, the bad luck that comes with being the weirdo named Lilac Skully.

"Well, I guess we'll see..." Christopher said. "End of the line's the old Church Cemetery down in Wormswood Village, and I've got a friend with a tomb there. Guess I'll be riding all night!" he chuckled, "Or will I?"

Lilac wished she'd never left home. But it was too late. The carriage had taken her miles. She'd made a terrible mistake.

She felt Titan's legs begin to slow down as they pulled up to the next stop. Stewart popped his head into the carriage.

"This is as close as I'll stop, Skully," he said to Lilac, "With the recent goings on, I'll not risk pulling the horse any closer. And I won't stop for long." He motioned for her to exit.

Lilac froze. *This* was her stop? She looked out the door. It was a section of pitch-dark woods lit only by the moon, with nothing else around—no buildings, no roads, other than the long, deserted Old Cemetery Road.

"It's up there to the left, quarter mile or so." He pointed to the right.

Lilac forced herself out of the seat. She wanted to beg Stewart to take her back to the manor. She broke out into a cold sweat as she walked purposefully down the steps, as if she'd ridden in the Carriage of Lost Souls a hundred times before.

"Thanks again, Stewart," she said. "I'll see you later, Titan."

The carriage door closed shut. Titan took off in a thundering cloud of ethereal dust. Christopher and the witch didn't follow her, after all.

Lilac breathed out a heavy sigh and took in a breath of cold, dark, midnight forest air.

9.

LILAC'S LUCKY BREAK

The clouds covered the moon and lit up the night with a dim glow. The road stretched straight and endless to her left and right, with no lights or houses or signs of civilization as far as she could see.

"You're okay, Lilac," she told herself in a whisper. "You've made it this far."

She walked in the shadows of the tall trees, in the direction that Stewart had pointed. She tried to find a landmark or something to remember where she'd come from, to get her bearings of which way was home. But it all looked the same, unfamiliar and dark. She continued for several minutes. An owl hooted in a nearby tree, and its deep, resonant call gave Lilac a shudder.

"Just an owl," she told herself. She remembered she'd read that owls were an omen of death in some cultures. She tried to forget that because she liked owls. There were all sorts of creatures living in the forest around her, she thought, trying to make herself feel better. It didn't work.

She saw something flicker up in the distance, and

a few steps further, she could tell it was the moonlight glinting off of a large metal mailbox—the only marker of a narrow dirt road that led deeper into the woods.

As she approached, she saw that the mailbox was marked with a tall, thin, sinister looking painted number: 11011.

She turned onto the dirt road, and the trees closed in around her. She stepped deeper into the forest. The owl hooted again, this time just directly above, and its voice sounded as if it were saying "No! No! No! Don't Go! Go! Go!"

Lilac felt a foreboding sense of doom, but continued forward. As she walked into the forest a few minutes more, the trees blocked the moon, and the dark of night grew thick around her. She thought about taking out her flashlight but didn't want to draw attention to herself in case there were things out there that hadn't noticed her yet. She continued in the dark.

The road twisted and turned a few times—unlike the Old Cemetery Road which had been perfectly straight—so she began to feel a bit disoriented with the direction and bearings she'd set. How far down this road would she have to go? Was this even the right way? She thought about turning back. If she went left down the Cemetery Road, she'd get home, right? She kept walking.

As the road turned one more time, something else

caught the faint moonlight in the distance. It was a chain-link fence, tall, with several rows of sharp, glittery barbs on top. There was an electronic gate with a keypad and maybe an intercom system that you could drive up to and press a few buttons to gain access. There was a large spotlight that wasn't lit up, and what Lilac thought might be a surveillance camera hanging off the very top. Lilac held back a bit, not wanting to set off any alarms. She stepped off of the road and into the forest.

She was almost invisible as she moved silently through the trees and shadows. Under the cover of darkness, she approached the fence to get a better look at the laboratory compound.

There was just one main building, with three identical white vans parked over to one side, all in a row. On the top of the building a large radar antenna spun around and around in a hypnotic way that made Lilac dizzy. Lilac tried not to look at the spinning antenna any longer. She sat down in the dirt and watched the building silently for a while. She took out the jar of water from her bag and drank some of it, ate a few crackers, and tried to write some notes in her notebook, but she wasn't quite sure what to say.

She scratched out the part that said "The Diary of Lilac Skully," and wrote, "Lilac Skully—Notes and Musings." She looked at her watch, then continued to write.

1:00 a.m. Made it to 11011 Old Cemetery Road. Looking for a way inside.

She couldn't think of anything else to say. Well, she could. But everything about the Carriage of Lost Souls sounded too fantastical and strange, and she didn't know where to start.

After watching for a while, she was fairly certain there wasn't anyone around. She crept up quickly to the gate to see if she could open it. She couldn't. She darted back into the forest. She followed the chain-link fence along the perimeter of the compound, but she didn't find any other spots where she might be able to sneak in. She tried to use her wire cutters to snip a hole in the chain-link fence, but as much as she tried, her small cutters weren't strong enough.

The laboratory building was a windowless warehouse. There were two roll-up doors on the back. There was a front door that was people-sized and another door on the far back of the building. She could see the air-conditioning unit on the top. She imagined Archie escaping from there. She sat down again, tucked in the shadows where she could see the front door, the white vans, and the gate of the chain-link fence. The silence of the forest and the intoxicating scent of the night lulled her to sleep.

Lilac woke up hours later, startled at the sound of a truck's engine. The first lights of dawn were just starting to color the sky a bright pink in contrast to the pitch black dark of the trees. She had been dreaming about having tea with a giraffe and two polite pirates.

She stood up and tried to remember what was happening, and where she was. She was in the forest. There was a laundry truck at the gate leading into Black, Black, and Gremory. She heard a beep from the intercom, and the vehicle went into gear. It moved forward through the gate.

Without thinking, she ran. She ran as fast as she could towards the truck, her legs, brain, and body just waking up from a deep sleep. Her muscles felt like they might tear, and she flung herself forward as the truck picked up speed.

She barely grabbed the bumper with her fingertips but managed to hold on. Her legs were dragging on the ground behind her in the dirt, but she managed to swing them up, and finally, get a solid grip on the back of the truck. She held on tight.

Her mouth curled up into a smile. She took a deep breath, a pungent mix of exhaust from the truck and fresh morning air. She didn't know if anyone had seen her, or where she was going, or what she was going to do when she got there. But she was a step closer. She was inside the gate.

The truck drove the short distance to the front doors of Black, Black, and Gremory, and stopped near the three white vans. Lilac did not hesitate. She jumped off the back of the truck, channeling the ninja movies she'd seen on late night TV. She scurried between two vans, and crouched behind a tire in the dark shadows.

The driver came around to the back of the truck just a moment after Lilac had disappeared out of sight. He unlocked the doors and pulled out two wheeled laundry carts. He rolled one of the carts to the front door of the lab and pressed a buzzer. Then he pushed the cart inside as the doors swung open automatically.

Lilac held her breath. The world turned upside-down, and she felt like she was floating, but she knew it was her chance. Lilac darted out and climbed over the edge of the second cart. She submerged herself under the piles of laboratory coats, uniforms, and towels. Then, she waited. Five minutes must have passed, she thought, ten, even? Still, the driver had not returned. She was beginning to wonder what was going on and jumped when she finally heard the door open. Laughter erupted from inside the building.

She heard the voice of the driver and another man approach the laundry truck. That second voice sounded familiar, and she listened carefully.

A sense of recognition hit her. It was the man she sliced in the leg with her sword. He wasn't dead! A wash of relief settled from her head down to her feet. She hadn't killed him. She smiled. She wasn't a murderer. She hadn't felt so happy in days. She didn't regret defending her home, but she hadn't meant to kill anyone.

The two men talked and laughed together. They sounded like friends, or at least, friendly, Lilac reasoned. She felt good. The air and laundry in the cart smelled fresh. Things seemed to be going her way already that day, and it was only just dawn.

The driver loaded the dirty linens into the truck and walked up to the cart where Lilac hid.

He grabbed the handle and began to push the cart towards the building. Lilac felt the vibration of the small wheels against the rough, rocky dirt lot as the cart started to roll.

Her eyes widened. She felt the laundry cart bump up to smooth cement and over the threshold of the building, onto an even smoother tile floor. She worried that the driver would feel her weight in the cart, but he didn't seem to notice. He wheeled her down the hall of the lab and continued his conversation with the man that Lilac had not killed, after all.

This was too easy, she began to worry. She didn't want to jinx herself, but she couldn't help it. It seemed much too easy. The men continued talking as she was wheeled effortlessly through the lab. She tried to pay attention to which way they went, but it was hard to tell from where she was. Left, left, right?

The cart stopped. Her breath and heart stopped, too. She heard a beep, and a door opened. The cart rolled a short distance and stopped again.

The men continued to talk and laugh and gab to each other, one on each side. They were talking about sports. Incredibly boring, thought Lilac. The two men went on and on, listing out endless strings of dull statistics and names that she didn't care to know. She hoped that they would just leave, but she had a sinking suspicion that they would not. They continued the conversation for what seemed like six or eight minutes, maybe more, which was forever to Lilac.

"Okay, well, I'll get your dirties out of here and see you on Wednesday, Bruce!" the driver of the truck said.

She heard a cart roll out, the light switch flick, and the door shut. The room fell silent.

Lilac couldn't help but let out a giggle of relief and disbelief. She covered her mouth and tried to stop laughing. This was serious, but it was also just plain funny. She felt like she'd gotten away with the easiest trick in the book. She lay there for a few minutes, wondering what to do next. Eventually, she felt for her flashlight in her backpack and turned on the dim light.

She took out her notebook. She looked at her watch. She wrote,

5:25 AM. I made it inside the building!!! More later...

The wire cutters had been be one of the most useful tools the last time she was in a tricky situation, so she pulled those out of her backpack and put them in her coat pocket. The box cutter might come in handy, too, so she put that in her pocket as well. She put the journal and pen back in the backpack, and she took another sip of water from the jar. She was getting hungry but knew it wasn't the right time to have a snack. She closed up her backpack, put it back on, and peeked cautiously over the edge of the laundry bin. The dim beam of light from her flashlight lit up the room. It was a storage room, with simple racks of supplies, linens, cleaning materials, and other things you might suspect to find in a laboratory.

Lilac turned off the flashlight and sat back down in the bottom of the bin. Time probably wasn't on her side. It was early morning still. She looked at her watch. 5:28.

She guessed it would be better to act quickly and be on the move, rather than wait too long and get trapped if someone came in. She needed to get her bearings, and then find her father.

She was in a pile of lab coats. Could it be as easy as getting dressed in a lab suit and roaming the halls in disguise? She giggled again. She turned on her flashlight and climbed out of the bin.

Lilac looked through the shelves of supplies and grabbed a paper mask, rubber gloves, and a white coat. She put them on. The coat fit awkwardly over her backpack, and made her look more like a hunchbacked troll than a laboratory worker. She found a blue elastic cap to cover her hair, and fit the mask over her face.

"Safety glasses!" she whispered. "Check," she said when she found them. She saw a box that said, "Booties," and took out two strange papery shoe covers, and put one over each boot.

Lilac walked to the door and turned off her flashlight. She put it in her pocket. She closed her eyes, even though it was pitch black, and took a deep breath. "One... two... three..." She counted. She pushed open the door.

10.

FATHER

The sound of her heart, a deafening thump, filled her ears. Without stepping through, she peered out of the crack of the open door. There was an empty hallway, brightly lit. She could go right or left but couldn't see what was beyond the twists of the hall in either direction.

She tried to remember how she'd come in—left, left, right—so which way did that mean she should go? She chose left but wasn't sure. She hesitated, and her feet didn't want to cooperate. She pushed herself down the hall to the left and tried to look professional, nonchalant, yet thoughtful, like she belonged there and was working on some significant research.

"Hmm, hmm, hmm," she hummed to herself a little.

She jumped when she saw her reflection in a stainless steel door panel. Her reflexes relaxed a bit when she realized it was just her, but then she felt embarrassed when she saw that she looked utterly ridiculous. The hump of her backpack rose up under the too-large lab coat that was draped over her tiny frame. The hair cap protruded from her head like a big blue bubble.

She continued down the hall. It opened up into a larger room with a wall of windows. Through the glass, she could see another room filled with weird-looking lab gear. Lilac stood on her tippy-toes to get a better look. She saw equipment that looked like stuff from her father's lab. Transceivers and antennas and all sorts of black and beige boxes with countless knobs and dials.

Her eyes lit up, and she stood the rest of the way on her toes. There, on one of the work tables, sat her father's pair of ghost communication devices—the ones stolen from Skully Manor. She was sure of it. She got a surging sense of confidence and excitement. She was in the right place.

On the other side of the room, she saw a door with a small window that led to another part of the laboratory. She tried the door handle, but it was locked. Not particularly surprised, she continued down the hall.

After a twist and turn, she came to another massive glass wall with a large room behind it. Unlike the previous lab, the lights in this chamber were off, but there was a familiar, eerie glow coming from the room. She stepped to get a better look, then gasped and stepped back. She felt cold and dark, and wanted to cry.

It was the ghost room, just as Archie had said. Row upon row of tall glass cylinders lined a warehouse room.

And in each one, Lilac could see the outline and the glow of a captured ghost, trapped and unable to carry out what they were here to do as they haunted the earth. Their glass enclosures sparked and sputtered, much more subtly than the horrible orbs that had kidnapped the ghosts of Skully Manor, but the same awful spark was still there. It was the sick, snapping electrical buzz that seemed to be an integral part of keeping the spirits trapped.

Her eyes felt like hot daggers were poking them. The sight and hopeless energy of the ghost room finally forced tears out of her eyes.

Lilac turned back down the hall. She stopped midway before rounding the corner. She thought about her father and concentrated for a moment. What he looked like, and what his energy felt like, from the little time they spent together, anyway, what his room smelled like, and what it was like going through his closet and lab. Then she tried to think—where was his energy in the building? She closed her eyes and put her hands out to her sides, trying to feel which direction to go.

She walked back towards the first laboratory. The hallway was still empty. She looked through the glass walls, past her father's equipment and through the window on the far side. She scrunched her nose. She was almost certain he was back there. She tried the door again. Still locked.

Lilac wandered back the way she had started, past the supply room doors and down the hall in the other direction. She passed another short hallway that looked like it led to some offices on the other side of the laboratory rooms. She followed the larger empty hall to see where it went. Back to the front door, she guessed. She was right. She rounded a couple of corners and saw the double doors of the lobby where she'd first rolled through in the cart.

"Well, at least I know how to get out of here..." she said under her breath. She was pretty sure that she knew the layout of the lab now and had seen almost all of it, judging from how big the building looked outside. It was a "U" shape, with a hallway that went around the two main rooms, and then the ghost room in the back, she guessed.

Lilac turned back towards the laboratory rooms but stopped in her tracks. There were voices up ahead. One of them sounded like the same man as before. Their footsteps and voices came closer, on the other side of the next corner. She stood and listened as they talked and laughed back and forth. She heard a door open and shut, and their voices grew quieter. She peered around the corner and could see the men chatting in a glass-doored conference room. When she was fairly sure they weren't looking, she held her breath and darted by. She picked up speed and trotted past the supply room and back to the central laboratory with the big glass windows.

She stopped suddenly and backed up around the corner. Someone was in there. And the previously locked door had been propped open. The excitement of getting a lucky break came over her again, and she had to contain a smile underneath her paper face mask. She crept forward again, cautiously, slowly, tiny step by tiny step to get a closer look.

The door was propped open with a bucket, and someone was inside the room, mopping the floor. The men's voices grew louder again behind her and it sounded like they were walking her way. Lilac took the chance. She darted past the mop bucket and into the laboratory room. The paper bootie on her foot caught the wet floor, and she slid. Her arms flailed and she struggled mercilessly to find her balance. She tumbled to the floor with an "oof."

They must have heard her—how could they not? She tried to remain invisible on the floor and listened to the splooshing sounds of the mopping and the very faint sound of music with intermittent, off-key singing. She guessed the person with the mop was wearing headphones and hadn't heard her. She felt the wave of panic subside.

"Hey Frank!" a loud voice called out.

Lilac froze again on the floor. Her limbs went stiff. Thankfully, she had fallen behind a large stainless steel work table, and the man who had appeared in the door could not see her from where he stood.

"Frank!" the man in the door yelled again.

"Yeah?" the man named Frank with the headphones replied.

"How many times have I told you to keep this door shut and locked!"

Frank made a noise like he thought the other man was stupid.

Lilac heard Frank walk to the door, and then she heard a beeping sound, and then a few more beeps.

She heard the door shut. Then the faint music began to play again, and the squish-squash sound of mopping started once more.

Lilac slowly rose up and around the side of the work table. She could see Frank mopping. His back was turned to her, and his headphones were on his head. Then something caught her eye. He'd left his lanyard and key card on one of the tables behind him.

She crawled on her hands and knees and scurried to the next table. The key card was still one table away. She peered up and peeked over the top, only to see him turn around abruptly and walk towards her. She jolted and flattened herself down, and held her breath. He set down a stack of towels. If he had been paying attention, he would have seen her—a little girl crouched on the floor, her frightened face barely disguised behind a laboratory mask and pair of stolen safety goggles.

Lost in his thoughts, the man named Frank turned to fill a supply cabinet in the other direction. Lilac seized the opportunity, and in an epic leap, she dashed to the table, grabbed his key card, ducked down as much as she could while running, and scurried to the door that led to the next laboratory room. She pressed the keycard to the sensor, and the door opened.

BEEP.

The beep couldn't have been any louder. It was the loudest "beep" in the entire universe, Lilac thought. She pulled the handle of the door and slid through it, as quickly as possible. She shut it behind her and wished with all of her might that she would find herself alone in this room.

But she was not. There, in the far corner, in a glass-walled cell with steel bar reinforcements, was her father. He was asleep on a small cot. There was an electronics workstation, a stack of equipment, and tiny bathroom facility with a light yellow curtain tucked into different corners of his closet-sized cell.

She froze. Her father looked thinner and paler than normal. His hair was disheveled, and she could clearly see the bags under his restlessly sleeping eyes. She realized she'd never seen him asleep before, or without his glasses on, for that matter. She ran to the door of his cell and put her key card up to it, but it did not open.

An alarm went off. A loud, frantic, blaring alarm. Lilac's father shot straight up out of bed in confusion, and looked out the window at Lilac. Lilac realized she still wore a face mask, safety glasses, and lab coat, and that her father probably didn't recognize her. She lifted her glasses and her mask. She called out for her father, who could not hear her through the thick glass. Lilac cried out for him again.

Shocked, he recognized her, and she saw him mouth the words to her, "Lilac, run!"

There was a look of fear and love for her that she had never before seen on her father's face. She saw in a flash how much he had missed her, and how desperate he was to come home. She saw him fill with panic as he motioned and pointed behind her. She heard the door open and the sound of men yelling close behind.

In the chaos and panic of the moment, as the alarms blared, a strange sense of calm came over Lilac. She got a familiar feeling that she now knew well—the feeling that a ghost was there with her, and wanted to speak to her. She turned and saw the apparition of the Blue Lady, encased in a glass cylinder, just as Archie had described.

Lilac had never seen the Blue Lady in her entire life, although the Blue Lady was a legendary ghost that had haunted the garden of Skully Manor and the woods nearby for several hundred years—maybe even more, depending on which legend you believed. She was an elusive spirit, rarely seen but unforgettable in the town's local history. She'd been ghost-napped from the Skully's garden over a year ago. But there she was. Her apparition was faint and weak, but she was still clearly present in front of Lilac. Her fists banged silently against the glass, and she motioned intently to Lilac Skully.

And Lilac did not have to hear her words to know what to do next. Lilac dashed across to the Blue Lady's cylinder.

"Get her!" the men yelled. The alarms were deafening, and Lilac thought her ears and chest were going to burst. Red lights flashed to the beat of the wailing emergency system sirens. Her heart started pounding along to the same thumping rhythm.

She jumped onto the Blue Lady's glass cylinder. Her rubber-soled boot got a bit of traction and she kicked off the thick, sparking glass tube. She grabbed onto the apparatus and swung her small body up and onto the ghost cylinder. The shocks of the electric wires stung her knees and pierced her nerves as she scrambled over. Yet she persisted. She'd been through this with the horrible orbs. She knew she could move through the electric current for a few moments, as painful and arduous as it was, and get to a point where she'd be standing on her shock-proof, rubber-soled boots. She rose up and stood, finally able to get a solid grip on the wires at the top.

The men yelled at each other confusedly as they tried to figure out what to do to stop her. Lilac took the box cutter out of her pocket, and she began to tear and cut and slash the tubing that fed the controls. One of the men pushed a bench over and climbed high enough to reach her. She instinctively kicked him in the face, hard. He fell back and grasped at his nose. Blood poured out onto the floor in big red drops.

Lilac gasped. She almost wanted to apologize for doing something so terrible, but she didn't. She was running out of time as the men secured the building and caught up with her ruse. She had no idea how she was going to get herself and her father out of this. But she'd exposed the wires enough on the Blue Lady's cylinder where she thought she could try to yank them all out. With both hands and all of her might, she pulled the bundle of wires and tubes out of the top of the ghost cylinder. Sparks flew out and a massive electrical shock sent Lilac flying across the room.

The world began to spin. Lilac saw purple and green and blue colors all swirling around. The blue turned into the face of the Blue Lady, who sang a funny song to Lilac.

Lilac Skully, a special girl
Lilac Skully, sees the ghost world
Lilac Skully, dance with me
Lilac Skully, I'll set you free
Lilac Skully, follow me.

The Blue Lady had auburn hair that was braided in a crown around her head. The rest of her wavy locks fell down around her blue robes—robes that shimmered like mystical silk folds from another time. Her voice was like a quiet whisper in the back of Lilac's mind—a voice of guidance that she always knew was there—but didn't know how to hear until now.

They were sitting on top of a rain cloud in a dark blue sky, dotted with sparkly silver stars. Lilac had a cup of strange tea that tasted like black licorice. It was in a delicate midnight-blue cup with cloudy white accents, rainbow trim, and a matching saucer. The Blue Lady waved Lilac forward, and she followed. Lilac giggled and hopped over clouds, trying not to spill her tea. But her foot slipped, and she fell.

The clouds beneath her slipped away. She fell and kept falling in an infinite fall as the world disappeared above her. The air rushed by. Her heart and guts were long gone, lost in the clouds far away.

Lilac fell into darkness.

11.

THE BLUE LADY

L ilac awoke and wished she hadn't. Her nerves felt fiery and jangled. She couldn't quite stay still, yet she desperately wanted to. The back of her head felt dull. And there was a terrible twist in her neck, as if her head had popped off and now sat at the wrong angle. She tried to move but found her arms had been tied tightly behind her back and her ankles, too. Her eyes darted as she squirmed and looked around in the dim light, trying to remember where she was and what had happened.

She was pretty sure she was still at Black, Black, and Gremory. She was on the floor of a small, empty room that felt similar to the storage closet. She tried to scoot towards the door like a caterpillar but made very little progress. She rolled over to get a bit more comfortable and to think for a moment. She tried to twist her arms back and forth, but she couldn't free herself.

Then she heard voices. They were faint, but she listened as hard as she could, holding her breath and closing her eyes.

"I don't like this at all, boss," a man's voice said.

Someone else said something, softer, much quieter, but Lilac could not hear what was said.

"Then what?" The louder man responded. "Then what are you going to do with her? Huh?"

A horrible feeling of dread sunk into Lilac's bones. They were talking about her. There was an extended, unintelligible answer from the other man. She strained as hard as she could and listened. She could not make out the words, but it didn't matter. She could tell from the tone and the bits of scattered sounds that it wasn't good.

"Someone's gonna notice that kid's missing," she heard the louder man say.

Lilac broke down. No one was going to notice that she was missing. Not anyone that was living, anyway, other than her cat, and her father, who was also imprisoned. The only souls that would notice were the ghosts of Skully Manor.

She lay in the dark on her stomach, falling in and out of sleep, her body aching and silently sobbing.

The voices of the men continued outside the door, for hours it seemed. She became hungry, thirsty. She had to pee. She finally fell into a deep enough sleep to where she was no longer in pain or conscious of her circumstances.

A gentle voice woke her up.

"Liiii-lac," the soft voice said. "Liiii-lac,"

She craned her neck around and tried to look up into the darkness. She could not see the apparition, but she could feel it. It was the Blue Lady. Lilac wondered if she was dreaming again, but it didn't seem like a dream. Lilac could feel all of the pain in her body. She could smell that she was here, now, still at the laboratory of Black, Black, and Gremory.

"Hi," Lilac said softly back to the ghost, not knowing what else to say.

"Thanks for getting me out of there," the Blue Lady said to Lilac.

"You're very welcome," Lilac said back after a slight pause.

"Stay still..." the Blue Lady whispered.

Zip! Lilac heard a sound behind her as her wrists freed up a bit. She went to release them the rest of the way, but a soft hush of the Blue Lady told her again to stay still. Lilac stopped moving.

Zip! Lilac felt her ankles now freed. She took a deep breath of gratitude, as the tape they tied her with had been pulling and pinching her skin raw.

Lilac then twisted her arms free. The sticky, thick silver tape was cut perfectly down the middle. She sat up to one side and pulled the tape off of her legs.

"Thanks so much!" Lilac whispered.

Lilac heard the sound of something tossed on the ground in front of her. It was her box cutter. She picked it up.

"I didn't think there was anyone in the world that would come for me," Lilac said to the Blue Lady, whose figure had still not yet appeared. "Why did you...?" Lilac asked in a whisper.

"You are loved more than you know, Lilac Skully," The Blue Lady said.

Lilac felt a warm presence all around her. She wanted to sink into it, just lay there and be hugged by it. Was the ghost hugging her? She thought so, but she wasn't sure.

After a few moments, the Blue Lady spoke again. "Let's go," she said, and Lilac got up.

Then the Blue Lady appeared faintly, just enough for Lilac to see her. She rose up and through an air-conditioner vent at the top of the wall. The vent cover popped off gently, and Lilac caught it.

"This way," The Blue Lady whispered to Lilac.

The vent was incredibly narrow, and although Lilac was quite small, she barely squeezed through. The ghost led her through a couple of twists and turns and then popped open another vent cover. The Blue Lady gracefully faded and swirled out, and Lilac came out headfirst with a thump onto the floor.

The room was empty and dark. Lilac followed the Blue Lady through the hall and out the front doors into the night. No alarms blared. No white vans sat out front. Everything seemed to be happening with a stroke of magic.

Lilac dashed behind the Blue Lady, running as hard as she could to keep up with the flying ghost. They came to the gate where Lilac had ridden in, and it slid open silently as soon as they approached. The ghost motioned for Lilac to hurry, and Lilac ran faster than she ever had before. As soon as Lilac slipped through the gate, it closed. The Blue Lady turned into the woods and motioned for Lilac to follow.

According to the Legend of the Blue Lady, if you follow her as she dances through the woods, you'll wander the forest till you die and become a lost soul— haunting there for eternity. Lilac wasn't sure if she actually believed that, but she felt a twinge of hesitation as the Blue Lady beckoned her to follow. Still, Lilac followed.

The ghost began to dance and spin ever so gracefully, her arms outstretched. Lilac could see and feel the ghost's exhilaration at finally being free, as she had been captive at Black, Black and Gremory for a very long time.

The night the Blue Lady was kidnapped from behind Skully Manor had been frightening, and Lilac remembered the incident well—even though her father had refused to tell her any of the details of what had happened.

She heard terrible, strange sounds of machinery, screeching tires, men yelling, and the faint sound of a woman's voice wailing just outside her window. Lilac had frozen in sheer terror. Later, she learned that the Blue Lady had been captured from the garden that very night. It had been quite some time ago, Lilac realized. More than a year, even two. It felt like forever. And to think the beautiful free spirit of the Blue Lady had been trapped in a glass cylinder that entire time. It made Lilac feel a little sick.

The Blue Lady gave another glance back to make sure Lilac was still following. Lilac smiled and waved as she ran to keep up. She followed the Blue Lady and they spun through the trees. The ghost's expression of freedom and happiness was contagious. Lilac began to dance as she ran. She jumped and smiled and laughed. The Blue Lady showered Lilac in a fine magical dust, and Lilac felt her feet flying even higher as she leapt through the air. Lilac spun and danced and twirled. The Blue Lady cried tears of joy, unabashedly reveling in the feeling of haunting the woods at the witching hour once again, as she had done for centuries before her capture and imprisonment at Black, Black, and Gremory.

Lilac began to grow tired and slowed down a bit. The ghost led her on a little longer and then motioned for her to stop. Lilac stopped, and she could see what looked like the moon shining off of the road up ahead. The Blue Lady walked to the road, and her translucent apparition flared brightly into full view.

Lilac gasped. The full form of the Blue Lady was exquisite—more than any legend could have told. Her hair and dress blew hypnotically in the breeze. She stood on the road and waved her arms gently. Lilac saw her call out silently, and then her apparition dimmed again.

Within moments, a familiar rumble made Lilac giddy with excitement, even before she realized what was happening. It was the thundering hooves of Titan. Out of the distance, down the long road ahead, came Titan and the Carriage of Lost Souls.

Titan slowed, and the Blue Lady motioned for Lilac to stay back. Before the wheels of the wagon had even come to a stop, Stewart flung himself off of the top of the carriage and towards the Blue Lady.

"Oh dear saints, Blue!" he yelled out, almost panicked and shaking, a tone Lilac had not heard yet from

Stewart. He grasped the Blue Lady around the waist. He picked her up. Lilac saw the Blue Lady fall into his arms and hug him tightly. He held her, and they spun around, spinning and spinning in a ghostly blur, the sound of their laughter carrying out through the woods.

"Are you alright?" He said, grasping her arms gently when they finally settled to a stop.

She nodded, and said, "Yes."

"How did you escape?" Stewart asked her, incredulously.

"With the help of Lilac Skully, of course," the Blue Lady said with a sweet smile and motioned her hand over to Lilac, who was hiding behind a tree.

Lilac ran from the woods and towards Stewart and the Blue Lady on the side of the road.

Stewart smiled at her. "Well, that'll be a bugger to Luther," he scoffed and laughed, looking back at the Blue Lady. "He's been trying to break you out of there for what, nearly two years now? And she's just six or eight years old and living?" Stewart chuckled and covered his eyes.

"Um, I'm nine." Lilac said. "Nine and three quarters."

Blue shushed Stewart. "I'll deal with Luther," she said calmly. "Which, speaking of," she sighed, then set a hand on Stewart's shoulder while looking down, "We need to get out of here quickly. I'm going to need to speak with him as soon as possible and update the Ghost Guard. There's a lot they need to know." She motioned back towards the site of Black, Black, and Gremory and sighed. "We've got to get the rest of them out of there, Stewart. We're running out of time."

Stewart turned the handle of the carriage door, and with his other arm, beckoned for the Blue Lady to enter. She floated inside.

"Miss Skully," Stewart said to Lilac and motioned for her as well.

Lilac stepped in. Other than the Blue Lady, the carriage was empty. Lilac breathed a sigh of relief. The door closed, and Titan pulled the carriage back down the lonely Old Ghost's Road.

Lilac couldn't help but find herself staring at the gorgeous, ethereal Blue Lady. The ghost looked back and smiled, wide. The Blue Lady was blushing, it seemed, as much as a blue ghost could blush, anyway.

"Thank you again, Lilac," the glowing spirit said to her, "for setting me free."

"Thank me?" Lilac said, "I should thank you! You freed me, too!"

The Blue Lady laughed. "I guess we're even then."

Lilac didn't respond with words but just looked on in wonder. Whereas the other Ghosts of Skully Manor had been haunting for a hundred years, Lilac knew the Legend of the Blue Lady went much farther back, centuries, even. And there was certainly a timeless, mythical, otherworldly look and feeling about her that was different from all of the other ghosts Lilac had ever met. Lilac was in awe. She wondered if the Blue Lady was special somehow. She wanted to know, but it didn't feel right to ask.

"It was the least I could do for you, and for your father." The Blue Lady said after a pause.

The caring way the Blue Lady mentioned her father made Lilac feel a sudden pang of eager hope, and her face must have shown it.

"Don't worry," the Blue Lady said to her, "we'll get him out of there, too,"

"We will?" Lilac asked. She felt silly, but she had to know if that could be really true.

The Blue Lady nodded, slightly, not much more than the raise of an eyebrow, but she didn't elaborate on how they would do it.

"I wondered about your name," Lilac asked.

"Some call me the Blue Lady, but most just call me Blue."

"I mean, your name before you..." Lilac stopped. She worried that she might have been prying and unknowingly asking something rude—but for some reason, she really wanted to know.

"Bronwyn," The Blue Lady said and then gave Lilac a funny look. "I never really liked it."

Lilac laughed a little bit. "Blue's a really pretty name," she said, hoping to make it less awkward. "Everyone missed you when you were gone," she added, "um, Milly and Bram and Archie said they did, anyway."

Blue smiled. "Bram's a dear friend," she said. "I'll be so happy to see him and the children."

The Blue Lady smiled again and wrapped her arms around herself. She sat back into the carriage seat and then looked out a bit into the distance, as if she didn't want to further the conversation.

Lilac sat back and closed her eyes. She felt safe. She felt loved, and she felt free. She didn't know what she was going to do next, or where the carriage was going. But for this moment, she felt as if she didn't have to worry. They sat in a warm silence, Lilac listened to the rhythm of Titan's hooves.

After a few minutes, she had to ask some more questions. She wanted to know so many things, she couldn't help it.

"What's the Ghost Guard?" Lilac asked. She figured she probably wouldn't get an answer, but she didn't know if she would get another chance to find out.

"It's an alliance that watches out for the affairs of the spirit world here on Earth," Blue told her.

"Do they guard ghosts?" Lilac then asked, feeling a bit silly but wanting to know nonetheless.

"You could say that," Blue laughed slightly.

"Because I'm worried about the ghosts at my house," Lilac explained, "they can't leave, and the people from the lab have come to kidnap them, twice." Lilac's eyes were wide, she wanted to tell Blue everything that had happened in the past couple of days. "And... I'm afraid that..."

"I know," Blue said softly, trying to calm her. "We're all in danger," she told Lilac, which didn't make Lilac feel any calmer at all. "But the Ghost Guard and many others are working to rescue all of the souls trapped in the lab. Your father's even involved in the plan," Blue winked at Lilac. "He's a smart man, Lilac," she added. "He and I have worked together for a long time."

"You have?" Lilac blinked hard at her. "What do you mean? You worked together? How? Doing what?" Lilac tried to get more answers but Blue wouldn't tell her anything else. Lilac's head burned with even more questions, but she did not press the Blue Lady. The carriage began to slow down.

"Where are we?" Lilac asked.

"The roadhouse," Blue said, more seriously, without having to look out the window to see. "I've got a lot that I'll need to attend to." She gave a smile to Lilac.

Lilac smiled back at her, hopefully, but Blue responded instantly to the thought that was in Lilac's head.

"You can't go back to the manor, Lilac," Blue said. "Not tonight, not even for a moment."

Lilac wanted to protest, but Blue's serious expression stopped her.

"You and I were fortunate to escape." She looked down, and then back up at Lilac. "The manor is the first place they'll be looking for you. And they *will* be looking for you."

"But where should I go?" Lilac asked.

"I don't know," the Blue Lady said honestly, "but not back to Skully Manor. I'll stop there tonight and let the ghosts know you're alright." She smiled again, but Lilac did not return it. Lilac's eyebrows were twisted up in the middle, and her mouth was slightly open as if she was in mid-thought, but the gears were stuck.

The carriage rolled to a stop, and the door opened. The Blue Lady motioned for Lilac to step out. Lilac found herself back at the roadhouse. She looked at her watch and saw that it was 3:33 a.m.

"Meet me here tomorrow night, before midnight, I'll know more then," Blue told her quietly.

Lilac nodded. She didn't have any idea where she was going to go.

"Can't I go back to Skully Manor to get..." Lilac

began.

"No, Lilac," Blue said, "not even for a moment." Blue's gaze pierced Lilac's, and Lilac stared at her, motionless.

"Meet me tomorrow night," Blue repeated, "and stay out of sight till then." Blue gave her a look just shy of a smile. Lilac nodded back obediently at the ghost.

Suddenly the roadhouse door swung open with a bang. Lilac got a strong scent of ghosts mixed with an exotic twist of cocktails, spices, perfumes, body odors, and the sweet scent of decay from several different centuries, drifting out on the wind from inside.

"Bronwyn!" a booming, brash voice called out, which shocked Lilac into a freeze. "How the flaming devil..."

A massive, dark ghostly entity flew out from the roadhouse and stopped midair when he saw Lilac and the Blue Lady standing side by side.

Much like Blue, this ghost wore clothes that looked like they weren't from the last several centuries—black, shadowy robes, which would have blended into the night, had he not been accented by layers of elaborate jewelry. There were several thick, heavy chains around his neck, amulets and crystals that hung down past his chest. Twisted metal bracelets wove all the way up his arms, and the rings around several of his thick fingers looked like snakes with jeweled eyes.

Lilac tried to stay calm and not show any fear in this specter's presence, but her body instinctively recoiled back with a shiver.

Stewart sauntered around the side of the carriage and stood next to Blue and Lilac, protectively, arms crossed, his eyes fixed on the tall, beefy, black-robed ghost.

"Hello, Luther," Blue said sweetly and stepped forward. She held her arms out for an embrace.

Lilac expected Luther's face to melt into a smile and reach out for Blue, too—how could you not? The Blue Lady was so kind and loving and just so beautiful. But Luther stood unmoved, and his eyes looked back suspiciously.

"How did you escape?" he asked bluntly. Although he was asking a question, it didn't sound like a question at all. It was more like a demand.

"With Lilac Skully's help, of course," Blue answered lightly, motioning to Lilac, and putting her warm presence around her again. "She freed me! Valiantly, I might add."

Lilac couldn't help but smile. Her… valiant! Although Blue had saved her in return, Lilac felt like maybe she really had done something gutsy back there in the lab. Since the Blue Lady had been captive for so long, her freedom was probably a pretty big deal to the ghosts.

"What?" Luther said incredulously.

The sharpness of the "t" at the end of the word felt like a dagger to Lilac.

"Are you that surprised?" Blue laughed, keeping her voice and demeanor light against Luther's darkness. "She's Marvin's little girl after all," Blue told him.

Lilac's mind started to go off in different directions. In the carriage, Blue had talked about Lilac's father as if he were smart, rather than just plain strange. And when she mentioned him to Luther, Blue called him Marvin, not Dr. Skully. They seemed to know her father on a first-name basis. Maybe they knew more about her father than she ever did.

"Get her out of here." Luther said. "Now." He spat on the ground, and then continued. "Extreme measures have been taken to keep this location off the radar, but there's no telling what'll happen if they follow someone *living* over here, she could blow the security of this whole operation." He shook his head and scoffed in disgust. "And meet me back at headquarters in an hour," he said to Blue. Luther spat on the ground once more and turned quickly. Then he disappeared into the dark after a few heavy, dusty steps in the dirt.

Lilac could tell that Blue and Stewart weren't fond of Luther, but they kept their cool.

"It's good to be back," The Blue Lady said with a big

smile.

She turned to Stewart, who gave her a bit of a concerned look from under his top hat. Blue turned to Lilac and knelt down a bit. Her flowing silk robes billowed around her in swirls and whirls that Lilac could have stared at forever. But Lilac knew it was time to say goodbye.

"Thank you," Lilac said, wishing she could stay with Blue, wanting to cry, but trying as hard as she could to look like she wasn't falling apart.

"Come find me tomorrow before midnight in the cemetery." Blue said to her. Lilac nodded. "I'll make sure the ghosts at the manor know you're okay," Blue added. Lilac nodded again and smiled, her eyes widening.

"Make sure Archie feeds my cat, okay?" Lilac reminded the Blue Lady. The Blue Lady nodded and smiled.

"See you soon, Lilac," the ghost said.

"See you soon," Lilac said back.

Then, Blue turned and Stewart followed her. They went into the roadhouse, and the clamor and raucous sound of the partying ghosts flooded out once again. The door swung shut and silence returned. Lilac stood in the dead of night.

Titan whinnied slightly and stomped his foot.

Lilac walked over to him and pet his nose.

"Thanks, Titan," she said. Titan nestled his nose under Lilac's hand. The energetic, spunky, funny feeling of Titan's ghostly head and mane made Lilac giggle.

The door of the roadhouse opened and shut again, and Stewart walked out.

"I reckon you better stay away from here now, Miss Skully," he told her. "Don't come back," he said, darkly. He gave Lilac a terribly serious look and then added, "They'll be looking for you, make no mistake. The living by day, and the dead by night!" he whispered the last part dramatically.

Lilac got goose bumps and ran off as fast as she could.

"Don't let your guard down, little girl," he called after her. Then his voice called out to Titan in a ghastly yell. Titan neighed and reared up, and took off in a thunderous cloud of dust.

Lilac found a dark shadow and stood alone. She wondered where she was going to go if she couldn't go home. She had no idea. She walked through the shadows of the cemetery, and hid between the graves. She could see the tall, rickety outline of Skully Manor reaching high up in the distance. It looked so dark and deserted. She wanted desperately to go inside, to climb into her bed, and fill the lonely old house with her presence. But she stayed back and just looked. She wished she had her crackers and jars of water. She was starting to feel hungry and thirsty. Her backpack was gone. They must have taken it from her before they tied her up in the closet, she thought.

She began to feel incredibly sleepy. She tried to stay awake where she was, silently watching her house in the night, but her eyes closed and her head bobbed forward and hit the dull corner of a gravestone.

"Ow!" She rubbed her head and her eyes.

She got up. She had to find a place to sleep, even if just for a few hours. There was only one place she could think of, and she walked there, barely able to keep her eyes open as she stumbled down the dark streets on the outskirts of town.

Creak. Lilac opened the small gate of the neighborhood park. *Clunk.* The gate closed behind her. There was a drinking fountain, so she drank for several minutes and filled her parched, empty stomach with the cold stream of water.

She climbed the ladder to the top of the playground tower with the tall, twisty slide. She huddled up, her hood tight over her head, and within two breaths, fell fast asleep.

12.

HAZEL AND FINN

"Lilac Skully?" a voice questioned.

Lilac opened her eyes. She tried to figure out where she was and remember what had happened. So much. She was outdoors. She could see the first light of dawn. She was in a park. She was at the top of a playground slide tower in a little hut. Who was there? Who had just said her name?

She turned over, flat on her back. Two figures peered over her with quizzical expressions on their faces. They both had shaggy, dirty blonde hair. Lilac thought she might be seeing double for a moment, but she wasn't.

"It IS Lilac Skully!" a boy's voice said with a tone of wonder. Lilac's brain clicked into recognition. *Oh god, no.* She thought to herself.

It was Hazel and Finn, the twins that had tormented her while she attended the public school for a brief time, years ago. It had ended badly for Lilac. And to her, Hazel and Finn were some of the worst and most terrifying people she had ever known.

Lilac jumped up. She was cornered at the top of the

playground hut. Without hesitation, she tried to plow between the two of them and dive down the long, twisty slide. But the twins were much larger, stronger, and well-rested.

"Stop her!" Hazel called, and Finn grabbed Lilac by the shoulders. "Lilac," Hazel said, more gently than Lilac could have imagined, "What are you doing here?"

Lilac stopped struggling and realized it was futile. She looked at their faces in shock and terror. But, for some reason, neither of them looked like they were going to hurt her or taunt her. Finn's hands released her shoulders. They waited for her to answer.

"Sss... sleeping?" Lilac said hesitantly. "Wh... what are you doing here?"

"Just bored," Hazel said, and shrugged.

Lilac looked at them with an expression that must have shown a lot of distrust and fear.

"Hey look," Finn said, casually. "I'm sorry about first grade."

Lilac's eyes widened with even more shock and suspicion. She pulled back.

"I really didn't mean to hit you," he smiled a little. Lilac did not.

"He felt bad, Lilac, and he got in huge trouble." Hazel said to try and smooth it over.

Lilac was not convinced. That was a defining

moment in her life. Hazel and Finn had been so terrible to her that her father took her out of public school, and put her into lonely, isolated, boring correspondence courses at home, tucked away in notoriously haunted Skully Manor. This incident with Hazel and Finn in first grade was not just something Lilac was going to consider glossing over and forgiving all willy-nilly.

"And besides," Hazel added with a little laugh and a friendly tone, "that was YEARS ago, Lilac."

Lilac didn't laugh, but she softened a bit. Her face and brows still wore an uneasy furrow. She felt that any slight twitch of emotion could erupt into a storm of feelings.

"I'm super hungry," Finn said suddenly. "I'm gonna go eat a bunch of cereal." He went down the slide.

"Come with us, Lilac," Hazel said.

Lilac froze. Go with them? What were they planning? Was this all a cruel trick? But she was starving. She couldn't go home to Skully Manor and had nowhere else to stay. Daylight was breaking, and people would be looking for her.

"It's okay," Hazel told her. "So you're having problems at home. Our mom will understand." She motioned for Lilac to go down the slide.

Lilac hesitated again. But she went down the slide a moment later, and Hazel followed.

Hazel passed Lilac and ran after Finn, not looking back to see if Lilac was still behind them, but she was.

Lilac ran after the twins for six or eight blocks. Her legs barely kept up with the larger, sportier children. They darted through alleyways and between houses in a zigzag path that only kids who knew the neighborhood would take. Eventually, they led Lilac down a driveway and past a small, square house with peeling white paint. Finn broke rank and went in through the back door. Hazel motioned for Lilac to follow her into the garage behind the house.

Lilac slipped in through the crooked garage door, panting and out of breath.

A bare bulb with a string illuminated Hazel and Finn's clubhouse. Old sofas, chairs, and furniture lined the walls. A dirty, colorful carpet covered the bare earth floor. There were haphazard piles and boxes of things stacked against the back wall.

"Have a seat, Lilac," Hazel said.

Lilac chose a funny looking turquoise tufted chair. "Do you want an orange soda? They're not cold." Hazel asked her. Lilac nodded her head. Her stomach bubbled and churned at the excitement of orange soda.

Hazel handed her one. "I'll be right back," Hazel said, and she left the garage.

Lilac opened the soda and looked around. She tried

to process what was going on. She took a sip. It was magnificent. Her hand shook as she lifted it back to her lips, trying to contain herself, but she gulped it down as fast as she could. Hungry and tired, she had a splitting headache. She could barely sit up. She leaned back in the chair.

Hazel and Finn came back quickly, each carrying a box of cereal. Finn had a carton of milk in his other hand, and Hazel had three bowls and three spoons. They set it all down on the table in the middle of the room.

"We'll have to split these two boxes between the three of us," Finn said. Lilac did not object. That sounded like a lot of cereal. She watched as they each filled a large bowl all the way to the top, then poured on milk.

"Dig in, Lilac Skully," said Hazel, through crunches of cereal.

Lilac grabbed a bowl and spoon and did the same. The cereal was like nothing she had ever seen before. It was a cereal that must have been specifically for Halloween. One was called Boo Berry, and it had a picture of a friendly-looking bluish ghost on the box and tasted like sweet, sugary blueberries. The other was called Count Chocula. Its box had a silly vampire pictured on it, and it was the most electrifying chocolate that Lilac had ever tasted. It was colorful and cheerful and crunchy. She hadn't had fresh milk in a long time, either. She started gobbling it up like a ravenous beast.

"You look starving," Finn said to her, as he crunched.

"You smell like pee," Hazel said.

Lilac did not want to look weak, but tears came instantly. She had been tied up for more than an entire day in the laboratory, and she had no choice but to wet herself after eighteen, nineteen, who knows how many hours, passed out and hog-tied on her stomach with duct tape around her ankles and wrists.

"Whoa!" Hazel put her cereal down. "Lilac, I'm sorry," she said.

Lilac was crying but did not stop eating the cereal. She crunched and sniffled.

"I was just making an observation," Hazel tried to explain. "You can shower and wear some of my clothes, and then we can wash yours," she offered. "It's really no big deal."

"I've totally peed my pants," Finn added without looking up, and shrugged his shoulders. "That's why I didn't say anything. So many times, actually," he chuckled at himself.

"Thanks," Lilac choked out as she continued to eat.

No one said anything else for a while. After they had all helped themselves to several bowls of cereal and polished off both boxes, Hazel brought Lilac into the house.

Lilac rehearsed her story in her head. If Hazel and Finn's mother asked, her father had influenza and had been unable to care for her recently, and she got locked outside and peed her pants. That was her story.

She went into the house, and her heart thumped. It was nothing like her house. This house was warm, small, and cozy. It smelled like coffee, cinnamon, and laundry soap. There was no scent of ghosts at all, whatsoever. None of the furniture was a century old. It was just the kind of house that Lilac had always wanted to live in. There were piles of clothes, haphazard bills, and trophies and ribbons on a shelf that had the names of both Hazel and Finn Cross.

"Mom?" Hazel called. Their mom was in the kitchen. "This is Lilac Skully, and she's going to take a shower here, okay?"

"Hi Lilac," their mother said, not even looking up from her newspaper and coffee.

"Hi?" Lilac squeaked out a weak hello.

Hazel stopped in the hall closet and pulled out a towel. She gave it to Lilac. "Wait here," Hazel said. She went into the next room and came back a minute later. She handed Lilac a long sleeved purple corduroy dress, some Christmas socks, and a pair of black sweat pants with elastic around the waist and ankles.

"Sorry I don't have much that might fit you," she

said as she handed the clothes over to Lilac. "These are the smallest things I have."

Lilac took them gratefully.

"This dress is... so pretty..." Lilac said. It was purple. It was corduroy. It was very much something Lilac would wear.

Hazel smiled and shrugged. "Meet us back in the clubhouse. Oh, and the washer is by the back door if you want to use it."

Lilac nodded. She went into the bathroom. The water was hot, and they had the kind of soap, shampoo, and conditioner that actually smelled good. Lilac was used to plain, terribly waxy bars of soap that her father brought home in bulk. It never really seemed to get you clean. And the kind of shampoo at her house was none at all, or a 2-in-1 that made your hair frizzy, tangled, and stick up in funny places like you just got hit by lightning.

The hot water of the shower washed away the intensity of the past few days. Lilac took her time. She looked around curiously. There was a rubber ducky. It was a real home, full of life and energy and love and living people. Their towels were fluffy and new. Lilac had never used a towel like that before. The ones at Skully Manor were threadbare, scratchy and stiff, and likely much older than Lilac herself. But the ones here were soft, warm, and fuzzy, like clouds.

She changed into Hazel's clothes, which were dreadfully large for her, but no matter. She used some toothpaste and brushed her teeth with her finger. She gathered up her dirty clothes and put them in the washer on the back porch. The laundry soap was the liquid kind that smelled like bright cheery sunshine and flowers mixed with fruit punch. She hoped her clothes would smell just like that when they came out. The laundry soap at her house was a chalky powder that smelled a little bit like sour milk.

Lilac went back to the clubhouse. Hazel and Finn were watching cartoons. They glanced over when she came in, but didn't say anything. Lilac sat in one of the oversized, stained, yet very comfortable chairs.

She settled in to watch. She noticed that Hazel and Finn laughed at the same times. Lilac started laughing, too. By the end of the cartoon, they were all in tears with laughter. Hazel brought out another round of orange soda, and Lilac drank it gleefully.

Another cartoon came on. It wasn't quite as funny, but the three children watched it and still giggled together occasionally.

"Soccer!" someone outside yelled suddenly. Lilac jumped back like a frightened mouse, but it was only Hazel and Finn's mother.

"Do you want to come?" Hazel asked Lilac.

Lilac's eyes became as wide as saucers. Her? To soccer? Lilac was not a fan of team or ball sports. She didn't want to be rude, but she shook her head and tried to politely decline. And more importantly, she couldn't be seen. Terrible people were looking for her, but she didn't want to tell anyone that, not if she didn't have to.

"Okay, we'll be back this afternoon!" Hazel said.

Lilac thanked them and sat back down with a wave of relief. She watched cartoons for a few minutes, then turned off the TV. She lay down on the lumpy, bumpy sofa and closed her eyes. Without the cartoons and the company of Hazel and Finn, Lilac began to wonder.

She wondered if there really was someone working to help her father and the ghosts trapped at Black, Black, and Gremory. She wondered what would have happened to her if the Blue Lady hadn't freed her. She wondered what would have happened if she had not freed the Blue Lady. And what the Blue Lady would have to tell her tonight. And what her father was doing right now, and if he was okay. And when she might see him again. She wondered how long she'd be able to stay with Hazel and Finn, unnoticed and seemingly safe.

Hazel and Finn. She still had a hard time believing it. They were the last people on earth she thought would ever help her. But now, they didn't seem to be mean anymore. They were fun and kind and had helped her out when she was in a tight spot. And they had even apologized for what had happened at school.

She thought back to that moment in the lunch room. They had said some terrible things that day. They called her a freak and a weirdo. They said things that made her very sad about her mom. But, she repeated to herself, as Hazel had put it so bluntly—that was years ago. And they hadn't said anything like that to her today. They had only been kind. But had they really changed so much, Lilac wondered. And why? How?

13.

THE PIZZA PARTY

She awoke several hours later to the sound of Hazel and Finn walking down the driveway together, laughing. Lilac was in a deep sleep and had to shake herself groggily, and tried to pretend to be more awake than she was. She had forgotten about her clothes in the wash. She got up and ran to put them in the dryer and greeted Hazel and Finn on the way.

The twins were cheering and high-fiving each other, and told Lilac how they had each scored some of the winning points in the soccer game. She had never cared for sports, but their energy and excitement was infectious. She told them they must have done a great job and gave them the most hearty congratulations that she could think of.

When Lilac got back from moving her laundry, Hazel and Finn had the TV back on and were drinking more soda. They asked Lilac if she wanted one, and she asked for water. They pointed her to the garden hose outside. Lilac went to the hose and drank out of it. It tasted like rubber and dirt, but it was cold and refreshing. Parched, she gulped as much of it as she could and filled herself up. She was hungry too, but the water helped wash it away. She went back to the clubhouse and took her seat.

A few minutes later, the twins' mother came in and asked what they wanted on their pizza. Hazel and Finn called out toppings. Mushrooms! Pepperoni! Sausage! Jalapeño! Olives! Salami! Lilac looked between them, blankly. The mother looked at Lilac. Lilac stuttered.

"Uhhh, anything, thank you!" Lilac said, not knowing what to say, and not used to having a parent that would order pizza or ask what toppings she wanted.

She realized her father had never once ordered pizza for her. She felt angry, but then she felt bad. He did deserve *some* credit anyway—maybe it wasn't pizza—but occasionally, if she asked him enough times, he'd order Chinese takeout. He even brought that home on her birthday, Thanksgiving and Christmas without her asking.

Thoughts like this had been popping up, in and out of Lilac's mind whenever she thought about her father. She had been upset with him, she now admitted, but it hadn't been entirely his fault. If she thought about it from his perspective, she felt sad for him. He was a prisoner, trapped, alone, probably worried sick about her. And she had been mad at him for leaving her. She flip-flopped between feeling sorry for him, and then back to resenting the deep loneliness as it crept back in. He hadn't been perfect, far from it. She'd spent much of her lifetime alone, she realized. Maybe he did have a hard time raising her by himself, but surely he could have tried a little more to make her feel loved—at least a little bit? She looked down.

Someone touched her shoulder. Someone was repeating her name, but she hadn't heard it.

"Are you okay, honey?" It was Hazel and Finn's mother.

Lilac didn't know how to respond. She wanted to say no. "Oh, yeah, I'm all right," she said, as normally as she could.

"Do you need to call your father?" Mrs. Cross asked. "About staying the night?" the mother clarified.

"Oh," Lilac said. "Oh oh oh, um, He's got terrible influenza?" she said hesitantly, and much more like she was asking a question than telling an answer. "I'd better not bother him, um, I already told him I'd…" Lilac trailed off. She was a terrible liar.

"Oh you poor dear," the mother said. "Well, you can stay here as long as you need," she added.

Lilac looked up at her and smiled and tried to mutter out a polite "thank you," but it got stuck in her throat.

The afternoon progressed splendidly. Lilac allowed herself to forget her troubles and watched hours of television with Hazel and Finn. Their mother brought in three hot, steaming, delicious pizzas with root beer and all kinds of toppings.

There were extra-spicy hot chicken wings with ranch sauce, which Lilac had never tried before. She was afraid at first, based on Hazel and Finn's reaction to the extreme heat of the spicy chicken wings, but they talked her into it. It was the hottest thing she'd ever eaten in her entire life. Her mouth was burning, and she tried to chug some root beer to cool it down. She loved every moment of it. They all laughed, and Lilac took another bite of the chicken wing, but this time dipped it in the cool ranch sauce. It was so hot, she had to stand up. Her eyes watered. Hazel and Finn laughed hysterically, each eating more chicken wings and having similar reactions. At the end of the feast, Hazel had been able to eat the most hot wings. Lilac's mouth was still burning slightly even hours later.

Eventually, everyone became bored and sluggish from too much TV.

"Let's ride out to the ocean," Finn said. He jumped up and grabbed his bike from against the wall.

"Okay!" Hazel grabbed hers. "Lilac, you can ride Finn's old one," she offered.

"I'll stay here, I... can't ride a bike, and..." Lilac tried to explain.

Hazel and Finn laughed. "You CAN'T?" they said in unison, and seemed to think that was unbelievable.

"No," Lilac answered, with a hesitant tone.

"Take this scooter then," Hazel insisted, and climbed over a pile of sports equipment. She pulled out an old pink two wheeled push-scooter with a handle.

"I've... never ridden one... I..." Lilac stammered.

"Everyone can ride a scooter!" Hazel cried, in a friendly yet slightly pushy way. "It's so easy! Look!" She tried to show Lilac the basics.

They took Lilac outside, and Lilac gave it a spin down the driveway. It wasn't hard. And, it was even kind of fun. Yet she felt uneasy. People were looking for her— dead ones and living.

But she wanted to go with them—badly. She'd always asked to spend time at the ocean, although her father wouldn't take her, even thought it was only a couple of miles away. Lilac thought about it for a moment. The ocean was in the opposite direction. She was already in a different neighborhood, and no one seemed to know where she was. She was with other kids. Maybe she could get away with a little ride and remain unseen.

"Do you have..." Lilac asked, not knowing what to call it. "One of those sports hats?"

Hazel burst out laughing. "A baseball cap?"

Lilac nodded. Hazel rummaged through a nearby

dresser drawer and pulled out a hat. It was blue and white with a colorful print on the front that said, "Seaside Fun Park" in cartoony letters. The hat was big on Lilac, which was fine because she was able to tuck her hair in and pull it all the way down over her forehead to hide.

"What, are you hiding from someone?" Finn asked.

Lilac tried to act nonchalant and say no, but she knew she sounded like she was lying. Thankfully, they didn't pry any further.

"Okay, let's go!" Hazel called out and took off on her bike. Finn followed. Lilac came next on the scooter, awkwardly, not quite getting the hang of it.

"Wait up!" Lilac called out to them. Hazel and Finn slowed down a bit, and Lilac went as fast as she could.

It was a ten-minute ride or so, and Lilac was panting, with one leg more sore than the other from pushing the scooter. She was huffing and puffing, but she was smiling.

The ocean was beautiful. The sun was setting, and the birds danced over the waves in a ripply, magical scene. Hazel and Finn put their bikes to the side and began to toss rocks into the ocean. Lilac didn't know why, but she threw some rocks, too. *Plunk, plunk, PLONK.* She smiled. *Plip, plip, plop.* She threw some smaller rocks.

Finn chased Hazel with a big handful of sandy mud.

Hazel chased him back, and threw some mud at him. He turned around and tackled her to the ground, yelling something like "Sea monster!" but Lilac wasn't quite sure what he said. They were both screaming.

Lilac thought about hiding, just in case they got any ideas about attacking her next. But Hazel started to laugh and to bite Finn's arm like she was a shark. Lilac realized they were just playing, and she couldn't help but laugh, too.

So maybe Hazel and Finn liked sports, Lilac reasoned, and maybe they played rough. And maybe they never read books and preferred to watch cartoons instead. But she liked them. She didn't understand why, but she was pretty sure that Hazel and Finn had become her friends. Friends with her—Lilac Skully—the strange girl from the haunted house.

The three children rode back lazily under the moonlight. The cool, autumn air filled Lilac's lungs, her mind swirling with new memories and relief from the lonely life she'd grown accustomed to.

But as the night wore on, Lilac was reminded of what lay ahead. She had to meet the Blue Lady before midnight, and find out what was going on with her father.

They ate leftover pizza, cold and stale like the

cardboard box it sat in for most of the afternoon. The children watched more TV and played cards and board games. The hours passed with lots of laughter.

Lilac looked at her watch. It was nearing ten p.m. She began to wonder how she was going to leave to meet Blue without explaining where she was going.

"Uh," Lilac yawned. "I'm getting kinda tired."

"No!" Hazel whined. "Come on Lilac, let's stay up all night!" Hazel jumped up. "Do some jumping jacks! Have some cola! Splash water on your face! Wake up!"

"Uh..." Lilac tried to think of what to say next. "I guess I can stay up for a little bit," she said timidly.

"We have to stay up at least till midnight!" Hazel pleaded.

"Midnight! Midnight! Midnight! Midnight!" Finn chanted and giggled.

"Uh..." Lilac didn't know what to do or say. She went along with what they wanted for a while longer.

They played the card game UNO, and Lilac was laughing so hard and having so much fun, tears were coming out of her eyes, and her stomach hurt from joy. Yet she began to grow uneasy about the time. She didn't want to miss the Blue Lady, and she couldn't stay up past midnight with Hazel and Finn, as much as they wanted.

"Uh... well, okay, I really have to go to bed," Lilac said, getting up suddenly and awkwardly. She tried to yawn and act tired.

"Lilac!" Hazel said. "Noooo! Let's play a different game! Stay up with us!" she demanded.

"I'm... I'm sorry!" Lilac said. "I really have to go to bed now, um... is there a place I can sleep inside?"

Hazel rolled her eyes and scoffed. "I guess so,"

Lilac didn't want to go. She was having more fun than she had ever had in her entire life. But she had to meet Blue.

"I'm... I'm sorry," Lilac said, her head tilted to the side. Her bottom lip stuck out in a frown.

Hazel shrugged. "It's ok. There's a sleeping bag under the sofa in the back den. You can sleep there."

Lilac nodded. "Okay, well... goodnight, um... thanks and um... I'll see you in the morning."

"Goodnight," Hazel and Finn said, disappointed.

Lilac looked at them. Her heart felt heavy. She turned around, and walked out of the garage.

She went into Hazel and Finn's house. She could hear their mother, Patricia, watching TV in the front.

Lilac found the sleeping bag and pillow under the sofa in the den. She set it up and found another pillow and a couple of books to stuff inside it and make it look like she was sleeping. She felt bad for tricking her friends, and she didn't think it looked very believable, but she didn't have a choice. She hoped they wouldn't catch her, and that if they did, that they wouldn't be mad.

She looked at her watch. 10:45. The Blue Lady hadn't given her a particular time. She had just said, "before midnight." Lilac wanted to make sure she was there early. She changed back into her own clean clothes from Hazel's borrowed dress and sweatpants and put on her coat. She folded Hazel's things and stuffed them inside the sleeping bag.

Lilac unlatched the door as quietly as she could, and slipped outside. She could hear Hazel and Finn laughing and watching something on TV in their clubhouse. The warm, glowing light from the TV illuminated the cracks around the doors and curtains. Lilac began to feel quite nervous and took a drink of water from the hose. Then she hopped on the scooter, and sped off into the night.

14.

INTO THE DARKNESS

By the time she got back to her neighborhood on the outskirts of town, it was a few minutes past eleven. She was still very early to meet the Blue Lady. She stayed on the dark side of the streets and circled around the back of the block, a little more confident on her new wheeled transportation. She rode over to the other side of Skully Manor and stood in the shadows. She watched the old house from a distance.

Skully Manor rose up three or four stories tall, depending on how you counted it, slightly askew—a rickety, ornate, and strange kind of silhouette. Lilac thought it looked lonely. It sure was dark, anyway. But within a minute or two, a familiar faint glow illuminated a window on the second floor.

"Bram!" Lilac said under her breath. Bram raised his pointer finger to his lips and held it there, so it was certain that he meant she had to be silent. She wanted to go into the house and talk to them so badly. Bram shook his head just enough for her to see his clear "no" and motioned for her to stay back.

Milly's apparition faded in next to Bram, then Archie's little sailor cap popped into the frame of the window, too. They waved at Lilac as their smiles faded into solemn expressions. Then the ghosts just stood there and stared at Lilac out of the window, and Lilac stared back. She tried to smile to show them that she was okay. Not knowing what else to do, Lilac waved goodbye and blew them a kiss.

She took off on her scooter and stayed in the shadows for the short ride to the cemetery. When she arrived, all was silent. Lilac crouched amongst the graves and waited. She checked her watch, and the minutes ticked away. 11:21. 11:32. 11:45. The Blue Lady said to meet her there before midnight, but where? And when, exactly?

11:50. 11:51. 11:54. No sign of the Blue Lady. Lilac didn't want to miss her. She left the scooter tucked behind the gravestones and scurried across to the roadhouse.

Lilac pushed open the door. There was a burst of strange glowing light, an unearthly noise, and the funny smell of spirits, spiced rum, cigar smoke, and wafts of strange perfume. She stepped in. There were ghosts and skeletons and creatures of all kinds sitting at the bar and tables. She saw something that looked like the spirit of a massive Sasquatch, and she stared at the huge, hairy creature. It sensed her eyes and locked gazes with her. Lilac couldn't help but show a shocked look on her face, then looked away from the beast as fast as she could, and tried to pretend she hadn't seen him.

Then, Lilac noticed someone else was watching her. It was Christopher Stefengraph, the tricky, drunk ghost who'd questioned her in the carriage ride. Lilac tried to pretend she didn't see him and slipped back into the crowd. She felt a panic rise. Others were starting to look at her, too. She could sense it. Lilac had her hood up, but she knew she still looked like a child compared to everyone else. And she didn't see the Blue Lady anywhere. She tried to get back to the door. Just as she made it to the entryway, someone's frigid spectral hand caught her shoulder.

"What are you doing here?" a voice scolded and shook her a little.

Lilac breathed a sigh of relief when she smelled the odor of hay and axle grease. It was Stewart. He pushed her outside. The carriage and Titan were out back.

"Have you seen Blue?" Lilac asked, trying not to seem frantic. She looked at her watch. One minute till midnight.

Titan stomped his foot impatiently and snorted.

"Not since last night," Stewart replied. Something about his voice was different. He seemed upset.

"Do you know where she is?" Lilac asked him.

A flash of anger passed over Stewart's face. He drew his lips together and didn't respond. Lilac gave him a disapproving look.

"She went back to Gremory," he said, his eyes looked down when he admitted the truth. "With Luther. I haven't seen them since. Doesn't look good."

"What?" Lilac gasped.

Stewart did not respond. Titan stomped and reared up a bit, ready to go.

"Hey, cabby!" a voice called. Titan stomped his foot louder with impatience. Stewart looked at his watch. Lilac looked at hers. Midnight.

"Just get out of here, Skully, don't come back," Stewart said, shortly, shooing her like a stray cat. "You're a fool to ever ride this carriage." He turned and called out, "All aboard! Last call, Wormswood Cemetery!"

"I'm coming!" Lilac demanded.

"I'm not letting you in, Skully," he said, his arms at his hips.

"Just try to stop me!" Lilac yelled as she plowed through his apparition. She opened the door of the carriage and jumped in. There, taking up an entire seat, was Christopher Stefengraph.

"You're a fool, Skully," Lilac heard Stewart say as the carriage door clicked shut behind her.

Lilac panicked. But before she had a chance to change her mind, Titan took off, and she was flung into the carriage. Then she saw a second passenger sitting in the shadows.

It was the same cloaked witch, Cerridwen, from the night before. Any breath left in Lilac's lungs eased out, and she felt sick. She had made a terrible mistake.

"Well, well, well," said Christopher, "looks like we've got the regulars riding tonight." He nodded.

Titan's hooves pounded the ground, and the carriage rocked this way and that for a bit before it steadied for the ride along the Old Ghost's Road.

"So, what kind of witchery are you two... hedge witches..." Christopher said and paused for emphasis, "up to tonight?"

The other witch laughed again. Lilac couldn't tell if she was laughing at her or at Christopher's attempt to cause a stir. Either way, Lilac was tired of the persistent questions.

"Like I said last night," Lilac said with a dose of guts that she pulled out of seemingly nowhere, "a witch's business is none of your business!"

The witch in the cloak burst out laughing again, gleefully this time. Lilac's face burned. That must have been a stupid thing to say, and she kept saying it.

"Leave the little witch alone," the old woman finally

said when she stopped laughing. Then, she laughed some more. Christopher looked up and around, trying to think of something else that was clever to say.

The carriage took an unexpected bump.

Christopher, the witch, and Lilac all had uneasy looks in their eyes. Everyone's face said the same thing: something was wrong.

There was another bump in the carriage, and a terrible growling noise came from up top. Lilac heard Titan cry out in pain. Her heart began to pound. No one said anything. Then she heard the sound of dogs barking and Stewart's voice.

"Hold steady, Titan! We're being hijacked! No, Titan! Noooo!"

Lilac heard Stewart wail once more, and then his voice fell off into the distance.

The carriage began to rock and bump so hard, Lilac thought its walls would burst to pieces. Lilac flung herself towards the door handle, pressed it down with all her might, and pushed it open. She let go and felt the wind catch her. She knew she was going to hit the ground, and hard, but she had to escape. Yet she did not. Someone grabbed onto her waist and jerked her back. She felt like the breath had been sucked out of her yet again. The carriage door slammed shut. Someone twisted her arms back. She screamed.

"Not so fast, doll!" Christopher Stefengraph said in an awful voice.

Lilac screamed again. She tried to flail. But the cold, dark, weight of the ghost held her down so she couldn't get up. And the carriage flew recklessly, faster and faster, hopelessly out of control.

Lilac heard Titan whinnying in pain and anguish again outside, like he was spooked and unable to stop or change course. The carriage crashed down a treacherous, rocky cliff. Cerridwen yelled out.

They flew downward at a great speed. The coach caught air, and Lilac's heart and guts fell up into her throat till she thought she might vomit. They hit the ground. Hard.

15.

The Underworld

The carriage began to steady out a bit. A pungent heat permeated the air. There was a dim red glow seeping in through the sides of the disheveled curtains. Christopher eased his hold on Lilac, and Lilac scrambled to the seat. One of the curtains had fallen off the rails during the wild ride, and Lilac looked outside.

They were in a huge cavern with yellowish rock walls. On each side of the narrow roadway, she could see steaming ponds of reddish black goo. Bubbles of nasty, popping gas rose and exploded every so often. Dark, shadowy, faceless figures lined the road and held up torches, hot pokers, and other brutal, mismatched weapons of war.

Lilac could hear Titan whinnying, protesting, and pulling back uneasily, but the carriage moved forward. And then, it stopped.

Lilac looked at the others in the carriage. Christopher had a broad, rude grin on his face and was looking right at Lilac, waiting for her to notice him. The witch was slumped over, not moving. Christopher swung the door open and motioned to Lilac.

"Ladies first!" he said. Lilac looked between Christopher and the witch. She didn't want to get out.

"Out you go, now!" Christopher said.

Lilac stood up and took a tentative step towards the door. With a ghastly foot, Christopher kicked Lilac square in the back. She gasped for breath and tumbled out of the carriage onto the rocky, steamy floor of the cave. As she tried to draw air back into her lungs, she saw strange tooled leather boots with excessively pointed toes. They were dark red leather with wispy, stitched flames in several shades of maroon and gray thread. The boots were walking towards her. She looked up.

She saw a tall, thin man with dark, slick hair, a pointy hairline, and a small, neat goatee. His precisely tailored suit was a deep red—nearly black—and the fabric seemed to shimmer ever so slightly in the light. He stood above Lilac, casually flanked by a pack of six gigantic black dogs with glowing red eyes.

"Hellhounds," Lilac said under her breath. There was no mistaking that these were the same dogs that had chased her a couple of days ago.

"Here you go!" She heard Christopher's voice say pleasantly from behind her. "Little. Girl. Skully." He enunciated each word precisely. "Turns out her name's

Lilac, not Lily, like she told me." He added, "She's a liar as well as a sneak and a scoundrel."

"Thank you for your excellent service," the tall man said. He tossed a pouch of coins to Christopher, who caught it.

Clink.

"Stay a while and enjoy yourself," the man with pointy boots nodded to Chris with a sinister wink.

"And welcome to the Underworld, Miss Skully, our guest of honor," the tall man said to her with a laugh. "You must know who I am?" he asked.

"Satan?" Lilac shot back, quick and cold.

The man burst out laughing and reached down to pinch her cheek. A hot rush of terror crept down her spine, but she didn't flinch.

"Not quite," the man chuckled and continued, "I am Forsyth Gremory." He seemed amused that Lilac didn't know that. "And this," he motioned to the dogs, who crouched and snarled at Lilac, "is my pack of puppies. Do you like puppy dogs, Lilac?"

She didn't.

"No," Lilac said. She knew that was the wrong answer, but she didn't care. Either way, this was probably the end for her. And she wasn't going to play games or beg for mercy. The dogs began to bark and snarl, snapping closer at Lilac till Mr. Gremory tsk'ed them back.

"What do you want with me?" Lilac said to him.

"With you? Why, Lilac! Don't play dumb with me." His face dropped to a menacing scowl.

Lilac didn't know what to say. She wasn't playing dumb.

"You've been up to mischief," he said to her. "Haven't you? And you've been making it much harder for everyone." He explained slowly. "Including your own dear father. Why," Forsyth Gremory added, stroking his goatee and pondering a bit, "if it wasn't for your meddling, we could have wrapped this up by now, and your father would have been home safely!" he laughed. "But now, look what you've done, Lilac!" He boomed. His voice rattled through the cave.

He continued. "You've caused your father a world of pain. And more importantly," he hissed at her, his eyes lowered and the dogs began snarling behind him, "your antics have derailed my research and wasted years of my precious time, and gobs of my money!" Beads of sweat began to appear on his brow.

Lilac felt both pleased and sick with dread that she had been able to derail his research so very much. One of the dogs jumped forward and snapped, nearly biting Lilac in the face. She let out a scream and scampered backward on the ground. Mr. Gremory called the dog off.

"You're here so we can keep you out of the way." he added, finally answering her question.

"And when will you let me and my father go?" Lilac said, as calmly as she could.

"When your father has completed what I've been promised." Mr. Gremory laughed. "Take her to her cell!" he called out.

The strange fiery figures with torches, pokers and pitchforks appeared from all sides. They were not human, and they were also not like any ghosts that Lilac had seen before. She tried to spin around quickly and squeeze between two of the shadowy ghouls, but they thrust their torches out, as a hiss of red hot metal crossed right in front of her face. She winced and jumped back from the intensity of the heat. Another ghoul jabbed a hot poker between her shoulder blades, and she felt a dull ache run through her body. She lost her breath again and fell to the ground.

She heard Titan neigh and rear up behind her, and looked back to see if he was alright. There was another group of fiery men surrounding Titan, jabbing their pokers and torches at him, too. He wailed and cried.

"Titan!" Lilac could not help but jump up and try to run to the horse.

"BEHAVE!" Mr. Gremory yelled, so loud the walls of the cave rumbled and shook. Bits of the reddish-yellow rock and toxic dust fell through the hot atmosphere. Lilac was knocked to the ground again.

"To your cell!" Gremory shouted.

Lilac had no choice but to walk in the direction that Forsyth Gremory indicated. She was surrounded by the ghastly gray ghouls. Gremory walked in front of her, flanked by three hellhounds, and three more dogs followed in the back. The procession walked about a hundred yards down a narrow path where cells with metal doors were built into the walls of the cave.

When they arrived at the door of one of the cells, a guard shoved Lilac inside, and the door slammed shut behind her.

The air in the cavern cell was thick and hot. Quickly, the heat became unbearable. Lilac was still wearing her wool coat and fall layers and could not keep them on a moment longer. She removed her coat but still felt the intense heat sinking into her bones and beginning to weigh her down into a groggy, foggy lethargy. She quickly became soaking wet with sweat, and parched. She didn't know how long she would make it like this. She found a bucket of water in the corner, but it was steamy and boiling.

Within a few minutes, she heard the rattle of keys, and the door swung open. She hoped they were bringing her some cold, fresh water at least. But instead, Cerridwen was dumped out of a wheelbarrow, still unconscious. The door slammed shut again.

Lilac didn't know what to do. She sat silently for a moment. She crouched down by Cerridwen, a motionless, cloaked lump on the floor.

"Hello?" Lilac said gently. Cerridwen did not move. "Are you okay?" Lilac whispered, reaching out with the slightest poke to the witch's arm. The witch still didn't move.

Lilac pushed on the woman's shoulder, having to use more force than she thought to roll her old body over with a half-thud. The woman's hood fell back from her face, and Lilac saw it clearly for the first time. She stared at the old witch, reading the details and years written on her skin.

"Oh, wow," Lilac said under her breath when she got a good look.

Cerridwen's face was leathery and wrinkled. Her features were exaggerated, her nose so lengthy and twisted, it went this way and that, then changed its mind and went back the other way. She had some warts and bumps, and weirdly long, wiry white eyebrows.

It was exactly the face you'd expect from an old crone witch. But Lilac could see the mystic wisdom and kindness upon it. The witch reminded Lilac of the wizened women from ancient Skully family photos. She wondered if Cerridwen had children of her own. She wondered what the witch had looked like as a child, and as a young lady, and if her hair had always been white. And Lilac wanted to know if the witch was considered strange by others for her entire life—like Lilac was. She wondered if she'd always been a witch.

Then, Lilac saw Cerridwen's thin, wrinkly lips move ever so slightly as she breathed out, and Lilac barely made out the words, "Hello, little witch."

Lilac stuttered and was about to talk, but the witch shushed her.

"No more than a whisper..." Cerridwen said quite softly.

Lilac crouched down, the witch's eyes were open just the slightest bit. Lilac looked into them. They locked gazes. Lilac suddenly became frightened. Was the witch going to put her under a spell or curse her?

The witch winked. Her eyes twinkled, and she spoke. "What do you say we get out of here?"

Lilac nodded. "How?" she whispered back.

"I don't know yet," the witch said. "Give me a few moments to rest and regain my strength."

Lilac didn't respond. She sat back on her knees. She felt beads of sweat dripping down her neck and torso.

"Were you playing dead?" Lilac asked the witch.

"Only halfway," the witch answered as if that was

a perfectly acceptable answer. Lilac wasn't sure if the witch was trying to be funny or not, so she didn't laugh.

"I'm so thirsty," Lilac finally admitted.

"Hold out your hands," the witch whispered.

Lilac held out her hands, flat.

"Like a cup," the witch said.

Lilac cupped them.

The witch's arm reached up and her weathered hand, fingers knobby and bent at funny angles, made strange motions over Lilac's hands. Cold, clear, fresh water began to fill her hands and seep through the cracks. Lilac tightened her fingers to keep it from falling.

"Drink it, quick," the witch said.

Lilac gulped it.

The witch cupped her own hand and filled them with water, then drank it.

"How..." Lilac whispered, dying to know how that was even possible.

"Elemental magic," the witch said quietly, then paused and breathed heavily for a few breaths. "A witch can harness the power of the air, earth, fire, water, and... herself."

Lilac didn't say anything for a moment. But she felt much better after a drink. Cerridwen's breath wheezed in and out with an arduous and painful sound.

"Can you fly on a broom?" Lilac Skully asked her. As

soon as the words left her lips, they sounded silly to her. But Lilac really wanted to know.

The witch chuckled. "With the element of air, my dear," she said to Lilac.

Lilac smiled. How exciting, she thought.

"But why do you ride the carriage, then?" Lilac wondered. Surely flying on a broom was better than that terrible, musty old carriage?

"Fewer bugs in the teeth," Cerridwen said, "easier on my old bones."

"Do you make potions with toads?" The question had been burning in Lilac's mind.

"Ah, it's been years, dear," Cerridwen told her.

Lilac wanted to ask if the witch had been following her, or if it was just a coincidence, but she didn't.

"Why were you laughing at me?" Lilac asked her.

"Forgive me," the witch said with a kind smile. "I wasn't expecting you to stand up to him." She beamed. "It was wonderful!" she chuckled quietly.

Lilac smiled.

There was a commotion outside. The ghouls shouted, and dogs barked and growled. In the distance, Lilac heard the wailing of a horse in pain. She knew it was Titan, and she felt so frightened and worried for him.

"Can you see what's going on?" the witch asked her in a hush.

Lilac went to the door of the cell. It had a barred window almost six feet up, much higher than she could see. But if she could jump up and grab the bars, maybe she could get a look.

She jumped and grabbed on, and her sweaty hands struggled to grasp the hot metal. She tried to walk up the door, but her rubber-soled boots slipped and slid in the humid, dank cave.

After falling to the ground several times, Lilac stopped to breathe and came up with a different plan. She rubbed her hands on the rocky dirt floor to get them as dry and grippy and dusty as possible. She tried again. With a running start, she jumped up, grabbed the bars and scuffled her feet up the door. Her boots finally gained traction, and she lifted herself up enough to see out.

Lilac could see a significant portion of the cave. There was a small army of ghastly shadowy creatures. They lined the roads and marched through in groups, carrying strange scraggly spears, pitchforks, hand-carved bows and arrows, rusty swords, and fiery, flaming torches.

Across the cave, at the end of a narrow path lined with bubbling brownish-orange goo, Lilac could just barely make out the form of Titan, whinnying and bucking up in pain. A gang of fiery ghouls and hellhounds surrounded him, and they were pushing him into a corral. Lilac wished she had her sword. Her arms began to shake from holding on, and she dropped down.

She went back to Cerridwen.

"There's a lot of ghouls out there," Lilac said to the witch, trying to be factual, yet the tone of her voice sounded worried. "I saw Titan," she whispered. "It looks like they have him trapped in a corral," Lilac said, unable to hide her concern for him. "Dogs were nipping at him and..." Lilac sighed. "I wish they'd let you and Titan go, they obviously just want me."

Cerridwen chuckled under her breath and then spoke. "A witch takes power into her own hands," she said. The old woman smiled at Lilac and added, "She frees herself. She does not wait."

16.

TITAN AND THE WITCH

"Well, then let's go!" Lilac said in an excited whisper. "Show me how to use the elements! We'll use the water to put out their torches. And we can use fire to melt the hinges on the door, and we can collapse the rock cave walls and crush them with the element of earth! And we'll free Titan and..." Lilac's eyes became wide as saucers.

"That's it! We'll ride Titan out of here!" Lilac said almost a little too loud, realizing she'd just come up with a plan that might actually work. She covered her mouth. She waited for Cerridwen to say that wasn't quite how magic worked, and that it sounded like a very foolish idea.

But Cerridwen's eyes lit up, "You think he'll let us ride him?" she asked.

"I'm sure he'll want to get out of here, too," Lilac nodded. "And, I think we're friends, I mean... I've talked to him a few times and I pet him when I could, and..." Lilac suddenly felt very childish and silly explaining all of this.

"Did you see any guards outside the cell?" Cerridwen asked.

"Not right outside, no," Lilac shook her head. "But there are a lot of them out there. A whole army!"

Cerridwen nodded and sat silently for a moment. She took a few deep, labored breaths and looked straight at Lilac.

"Ready to go now, then?" the witch smiled.

Lilac nodded and stood up. Cerridwen held out her hand. Lilac helped her get to her feet. The old woman was heavier, slower, and less steady than Lilac had imagined.

"Get your coat," Cerridwen said bluntly, and in the same step, held out her hand, pointed at the door, and shot a powerful blast of lightning where the lock sat on the other side. There was a clink when the lock fell, and the door popped open an inch or two.

"Where's the horse?" Cerridwen said as she looked back at Lilac.

"Straight across," Lilac pointed.

Limping terribly side to side, her clenched fists exaggerating the pain and difficulty in her gait, Cerridwen walked out the door as if she owned the place. She marched right out in the center of the rocky path, hobbled and slow. Her shoulders moved in a grinding motion, and her face winced to help her keep her balance and push forward. Lilac followed.

Lilac heard the hellhounds begin to bark, and the ghouls yelling up ahead. She pulled her black hood over her head, just like Cerridwen.

Bam!

Lilac ducked instinctively and gasped. Cerridwen had raised an arm, and a tumble of rocks fell from the ceiling of the cave.

Bam!

Cerridwen sent another load of rocks falling. Her fists clenched as she limped forward, painfully, stopping only to carry out the third blast of rocks.

"Go ahead and get the horse," she wheezed to Lilac, seemingly already losing much of her power, mobility, and breath. "I'll hold them off here."

Cerridwen sat down awkwardly against one of the large boulders and breathed in a heavy full-body gasp.

Lilac did not hesitate, but she didn't know what she was going to do, either. She could see Titan up ahead in a large corral. There were three hellhounds snarling at him and keeping guard. She heard another blast behind her. Cerridwen's arms rose up. A giant wave of hot molten goo rose up from the steaming pool nearby. It crashed down over a gang of ghastly demon guards, knocking them down and sweeping them out into the red-hot lakes.

Lilac felt the flaming torch bearers screech up behind her in a hissing, sizzling heat. A torch swipe singed her back. She tried not to look, but she did. A pack of six spooks were gaining on her.

Then, a sudden gust of wind came roaring through the cave. The heat on her heels dissipated, and the flaming men and their torches were snuffed out by the wind.

"The power of air," Lilac said to herself and tried to feel the air propelling her under her feet as she ran as fast as she could.

She was almost to the corral. She focused. The dogs ahead hadn't noticed her yet. But she was running straight for them. She leaped and flung herself over the gate and into the corral.

"Aaaah!" She screamed as a dog's jaw latched onto her foot and bit down, hard. The dog twisted its jaws. Lilac kicked back, harder. The dog fell away, but another jumped over the gate and came straight for her.

She lunged for a shovel propped against the corral wall and smashed the hellhound's temple as hard as she could. He fell back in a whimper. She shuddered.

"Sorry!" she said under her breath.

Titan reared up in a panic. He was gigantic. His back towered over Lilac, and his head seemed three-times her height. He kicked his forceful back legs towards her in the small cell, and she threw herself out of his way just in time. She could hear the yelling and snarling of more ghouls and dogs approaching.

Lilac didn't know how she was going to get herself up on Titan's back and ride him, let alone how she would hoist Cerridwen up to ride with her. And she didn't even know if she would be able to ride the horse at all. He was a ghost-horse, and she might fall right through him. She wasn't really sure. She started to feel sick and incredibly foolish. What if this didn't work?

But Lilac didn't have any more time to think. There was no backup plan. She darted back to where she had picked up the shovel and grabbed an old broom from against the corral wall. She jumped with both feet onto the gate, then twisted backward, and leaped off again. She barely got a grip onto Titan with her free hand, yanking his mane as she scrambled and struggled to hold on.

The ghost horse reared up again in fright and kicked wildly. Lilac swung back and forth, barely keeping a grasp on his mane. She managed to pull herself up as the horse continued to struggle and buck.

More hellhounds surrounded the corral, and Lilac could see a pack of shadowy torchbearers closing in ahead.

"Go! Titan! Run!" she yelled as she steadied herself

on his back. He reared up again and tried to buck her off, and she almost lost her grip once more. Lilac hung on for dear life with one hand and all of the other muscles in her legs and body, the broom tucked tightly under her arm and other hand.

She closed her eyes. "Titan, run!" she whispered, this time as softly and gently as she could. "Let's get out of here! Please!" She said, holding onto his neck with one arm like a hug. She spoke to him without words, using the feelings inside her instead. He reared up one more time and with an ear-splitting roar, kicked his powerful front feet. Lilac saw the hellhounds fly out in all directions, as the gate of the corral shattered with a spark and bang of electricity.

Titan's hooves dug into the cave floor, and he picked up speed. Rocks fell all around, as the ceiling of the cave began to shatter and weaken.

"Cerridwen!" Lilac called out, and leaned over the horse. She held out the broom.

The witch whooped and hollered when she saw the broom, and stood up, slowly, painfully, and raised her arms to catch it.

Lilac leaned down over the side of the horse. "Catch!" she yelled as she tossed the broomstick to the beckoning Cerridwen. Lilac tried to toss it as gently as possible, but the force of Titan's speed made the release of the broom more of a hard *thwack*.

Lilac tried to look back. She couldn't tell if Cerridwen had caught it, or if the old woman was struck in the head with it. Titan's speed increased. Lilac became very worried. She tried to get Titan to stop or slow down and make sure the witch was following, but he would not. She tried to look back again, but Titan was running at full gallop, and any movement or shift of balance would send Lilac slipping off of his back. She held onto the horse with her arms and legs, hoping with all her might that the old witch was following behind on the broom. Warm air rushed by in a sweaty, sticky heat. Lilac could barely hold on to the apparition of the horse.

Titan began to climb the hill that the carriage had crashed down. As the grade steepened, Lilac's hands slipped more. All of her limbs shook as she felt her grip loosen. Titan charged ahead, faster and faster through the damp, hot air. She felt herself slipping backward more, millimeter by millimeter, as Titan's silvery mane and hair slid beneath her. Her legs began to feel weak, and her fingers tightened like they were going to bend back over themselves and stay stuck that way forever.

Finally, her lungs caught a cold, fresh, blast of forest air. Titan roared and whinnied in a wail of freedom. He slowed down enough for Lilac to get a better grip.

Then, with a whoosh and a glorious cackling laugh,

Cerridwen swooped by on the broom. She shot up into the sky and blasted a trail of shining, shimmering, starry dust behind her.

"Woooo!" Lilac yelled into the dead of night. She raised a fist into the air, with Titan's ghostly hooves galloping beneath her.

Cerridwen circled back and whizzed by again, then slowed her speed to fly alongside. Lilac could see a bright smile twinkling in the witch's deep eyes.

"See you around, little witch!" Cerridwen called out to Lilac as she zoomed off into the night.

17.

THE END

L ilac sat back and loosened her grip. She smiled. Titan's pace had steadied and calmed down, and Lilac felt more comfortable as he galloped along. The trees and forest began to look a bit more familiar, and she was pretty confident they were back on the Old Ghost's Road. Lilac took a deep breath of relief, and let the wild, free motion of riding the horse take over.

But as she approached the roadhouse, she felt she hadn't accomplished anything that night, other than getting herself into serious trouble. She hadn't found the Blue Lady. Her father was still imprisoned. She'd probably almost died or at least practically gotten herself locked in the underworld forever.

She saw a group of figures standing together behind the roadhouse. What if it was Gremory? What if it was another trap for her kidnapping? Her pulse quickened again. She tried to get Titan to slow down so she could see who it was, but he would not.

Titan screeched to a halt at the roadhouse and let out an exhausted sigh. His horsey knees buckled under him. Lilac tumbled off and skidded across the rocky dirt with a bit of a thud.

"Titan!" Stewart exclaimed, rushing to his horse's side. The gigantic ghost horse sighed and lay his head on Stewart's shoulder.

Lilac got to her feet.

"Blue!" she exclaimed, seeing the figure of the beautiful ghost standing nearby. "I couldn't find you! And..." Lilac tried to explain what had just happened, but she was at a loss for words.

"I'm so glad you're okay," Blue floated forward and reached out to embrace Lilac. "Still alive, it looks like."

Lilac nodded and smiled at Blue.

"Get her out of here," Luther said as he stepped forward.

His apparition in black robes was barely visible in the night—although Lilac could sense his unsettling presence and see a glint of his jewelry.

"Now!" Luther roared. A sudden, forceful wind picked up through the neighborhood and knocked Lilac back into a shadow on the ground.

The crowd of other ghosts around them dissipated. Stewart got Titan to his feet and led him back towards the Old Ghost's Road.

"Tell me what's going on with my father," Lilac demanded as she stood up to meet Luther face to face, determined not to let him intimidate her.

"I have a letter for you, from him," The Blue Lady replied before Luther could answer, and she pulled a small folded scrap of paper out of her pocket.

"You went back for him?" Lilac jumped up in excitement. "When? What happened? Where is he?" Lilac tried to ask, but Blue stopped her.

Lilac read the letter. In her fathers unmistakable scraggly, scratchy, uneven, and almost unreadable handwriting it said,

> *My dearest Lilac,*
>
> *Do not return home to Skully Manor under any circumstances. I have made arrangements for you to stay with the Mulligans until my release.*
>
> *With any luck, just another couple of weeks.*
>
> *Yours, Father.*

"What?" Lilac said. "I'm going to stay with the Mulligans? For a couple of weeks? I barely know them! This is nuts!"

Blue laughed. "He's *your* father, dear. And he's been worried sick about you."

Lilac read the whole thing once or twice with a skeptical look on her face, but she read the beginning and end over and over several more times.

"My dearest Lilac," and, "Yours, Father," it said. Her heart thumped. *Dearest Lilac.* He'd never said that or written that to her, as much as she'd wanted him to.

She clutched the note to her chest. His dearest. She smiled. She thought about how sad she had been to see him locked up and how much she missed him. And how she could see it in his eyes at the laboratory—he did love her after all, and he missed her too. Very much.

She looked up at the Blue Lady. The note said she was going to stay with the Mulligans, but did that mean right now? At their house? And for a couple of weeks? That sounded like forever. The Mulligans were a nice enough couple, although Lilac had only met them once or twice. They were amateur ghost investigators who knew her father. On one occasion, they had run screaming from Skully Manor when an investigation ended with a frightening poltergeist encounter. Lilac tried to figure out why she would be going to stay with them, and what they had to do with everything going on.

"The Mulligans are some of the living that work with the Ghost Guard," Blue explained without Lilac having to ask. "So they know..."

"Enough." Luther cut her off. "Get that little girl back to the world of the living. Now!"

"Do the Mulligans know about my father? Will

they tell me more about what's going on?" Lilac asked, ignoring Luther.

Blue held out her hand.

"Now!" Luther hissed again.

"Let's go, Lilac," Blue said.

Lilac wanted to know more, but she knew it was not the time.

"Can we get my scooter?" Lilac pointed to the cemetery across the way where she'd hidden it. She knew it wasn't hers. She'd borrowed it from Hazel and Finn, and a bit of a worried feeling began to wash over her. She hoped they wouldn't be mad. She'd just run out in the night and had stolen their scooter without explanation, and after they had been so kind to her.

"Yes, but we've got to move quickly," the Blue Lady said with a whisper.

Lilac ran to the scooter and hopped on, then followed Blue through the cemetery, and out into the neighborhood on the edge of town.

In a way, Lilac thought to herself as she rode along, she'd succeeded. She *did* find her father. She knew exactly where he was, even if he hadn't been freed yet. She smiled. And she had a message from him with an update. He'd thought about her and somehow arranged a place for her to stay. And the note said, "My dearest Lilac."

Lilac's face beamed. She scooted along, lost in her thoughts, following the Blue Lady as she danced and twirled through the winding side streets of town.

Then Blue slowed down and ducked into the shadows of a small front yard.

"This is it," she whispered to Lilac.

Lilac looked at the house. It looked cozy enough, but it was pitch black. She looked at her watch. 3 a.m.

"Are they expecting me?" Lilac asked Blue.

"Yes," Blue assured her. "Knock on the door. I'll wait till you get in and wave so they know I'm here."

"Where are you going? How will I find you again?" Lilac asked, feeling as if she was being too forward now, but not wanting to lose contact with the only one who seemed to know what was going on with her father.

"I'll be in touch with the Mulligans, and I'll stop by to see you in a few nights," Blue said. "And I'll go by Skully Manor before dawn, to let your friends know where you are and tell them that you're okay," she added.

Lilac nodded. She wanted to go home to Skully Manor, too. She pulled the note from her father out of her pocket again, just to be sure. It was his strange, unreplicable handwriting, and it said he wanted her to stay with the Mulligans, whatever the reason.

"Will you make sure Archie feeds my cat?" Lilac asked urgently. "He knows how to do it. There should be enough kibble for a while..."

Blue smiled and nodded. "See you soon, Lilac," she said.

"See you soon," Lilac said to the Blue Lady, although she wanted to say much more. Lilac stashed the scooter in the bushes and went to the door of the house. She knocked softly.

Within a few seconds, it opened up. It was SueAnn Mulligan. She was wearing a fluffy pink robe and had a sleepy look on her face. She motioned for Lilac to come in and waved to Blue. Lilac looked back and saw Blue's apparition disappear into the dark of the night.

Although it seemed safe enough, it felt uncomfortable for Lilac to be in the Mulligans' house. She really didn't know them at all. SueAnn hung up Lilac's coat and gave her a plate of cookies, milk, and cheese. Lilac felt awkward, but she was more hungry than anything, so she ate it all as she pressed for information about her father, the Ghost Guard, and the Blue Lady.

SueAnn told her they would talk in the morning, since it was well past 3 a.m, and she was tired. Lilac didn't question her further, but she did ask for more cookies and milk.

There were clean pajamas and clothes set out for Lilac and a brand new toothbrush. Lilac took a hot shower and wondered how long the Mulligans had been expecting her to show up. It felt strange to be at someone's house that she didn't know, but she was comforted by the fact that her father had planned out a safe place for her to stay. She put on the warm new pajamas. They were purple with drawings of white kittens on them. Lilac had never worn anything so cute before in her life, and she loved it.

SueAnn showed Lilac to a small, plain back bedroom and asked her if she needed anything else. Lilac asked for a big glass of water, a pen, and a notebook. SueAnn got her the things she wanted and told her not to worry.

Lilac nodded her head. She decided she liked SueAnn well enough and wondered if SueAnn had picked out the purple kitten pajamas. If so, she had made an excellent choice.

As soon as SueAnn closed the door, Lilac opened the notebook.

Notes and Musings Part 2

By Lilac Skully

She wrote at the top, since she had lost her first notebook at Black, Black, and Gremory. So much had happened since then. But she felt too tired to write it all down. She could write more tomorrow, she figured. She took the pen and wrote just a few short lines:

4 a.m.
I found my father!
And I finally rode a horse.
A ghost horse.

There was so much more she wanted to write, but her eyelids were too heavy to keep them open. She lay back in the bed. It was unfathomably comfortable. Much more comfortable than the ancient, lumpy mattresses at Skully Manor. She switched off the lamp on the bedside table.

Just as she closed her eyes, she heard a familiar rustle and huff outside the window. There was a faint bluish green glow.

She sat up and peered out. It was Titan. He nodded his head, and she swore he winked his eye at her and said, "Thank you."

"Thank you, Titan," she whispered back, holding her hand up to the glass. "I'm glad we're friends."

Titan reared up and whinnied in a mighty roar, then took off into the night. Lilac closed her eyes and smiled as she listened to the sound of his thunderous hooves fade off into the distance.

A Note from Amy:

Dear Reader, I hope you enjoyed *Lilac Skully and the Carriage of Lost Souls!* I love stories about shy, imperfect heroines succeeding in impossible tasks at the very last minute. And I find that things often work out that way in real life, too, especially when your heart is in the right place.

My favorite part of this book was writing the details of the various ghosts and haunted locations, like Luther, the roadhouse, and the third floor of Skully Manor.

The world of spirits is very much alive in Lilac's town of Steamville, and she'll visit the most haunted location yet as she sets off on her third adventure! There's trouble brewing at the local seaside amusement park... and Lilac is the only one who can save the night.

Don't miss Lilac's third book, *Lilac Skully and the Halloween Moon!*

And if you'd like to leave a review of this book and share your thoughts with other readers, it would be much appreciated.

Thanks for reading!

Amy Cesari

The Lilac Skully Series

About the Author

Amy Cesari is an author and illustrator who lives in an enchanted forest. She enjoys growing pumpkins in the summer, crocheting in the winter, and watching cartoons year-round. She believes in magic and in the power of following your own creativity. And she has every Nintendo game console ever made, plus a vintage Ms. PacMan arcade machine.

You can contact Amy at: amy@lilacskully.com or visit LilacSkully.com for a spooky surprise.

Made in the USA
Middletown, DE
12 November 2018